The Troublesome Mr. Collins

A Pride and Prejudice Variation

Linda C. Thompson

The Troublesome Mr. Collins - A Pride and Prejudice Variation
First Edition

For information, please contact:
Linda C. Thompson Books
1700 Lynhurst Lane
Denton, TX 76205

Cover Template: Lori Whitlock (www.loriwhitlock.com)
Cover Design: Linda C. Thompson
Cover Photo & Graphic Flourish: Depositphotos.com
Photo By: @flotsom
Flourish By: @PinkPueblo

ISBN-13: 978-1-7332420-2-8
ISBN-10: 1-7332420-2-3

DEDICATION

To Debbie, my partner in my crime for as long as I can remember. Our friendship has stood the test of time. I love you, sister of my heart, and always will!

TABLE OF CONTENTS

A BREAK FROM UNWANTED ATTENTIONS

THE WET GRASS SPARKLED IN THE bright light of the late autumn sun. The air smelled of damp earth and was brisk and refreshing. Water dripped from the leafless branches, leaving puddles to avoid at every turn. However, after several days of being confined to the house with her fractious sisters and their unwanted guest, Elizabeth desperately needed the comfort of a walk in nature to find the peace to return home.

"Cousin Elizabeth, you must wait. It is not appropriate for a young lady to walk about the countryside unattended." Gasping breaths punctuated Mr. Collins' words. No reply came. The young lady to whom he wished to propose was nowhere to be seen. "Cousin Elizabeth," he called again. "I have something important to discuss with you. Please come back."

Elizabeth Bennet kept her head down and her eyes on the path. She hurried away from her companion as rapidly as her feet could carry her while trying to make as little noise as possible. The portly parson would be unable to keep up. If fortune favored Elizabeth, he would quickly give up his pursuit. With any luck, she would be able to sneak into the house and up to her room with only enough time to change for the Netherfield ball that evening, thereby avoiding her cousin's officious attentions.

Reaching her destination, Elizabeth settled down on her favorite rock atop of Oakham Mount and stared out over Netherfield Park and the village of Meryton. In the opposite direction, her father's estate was visible. She had no desire to gaze upon it at present.

Catching her breath, Elizabeth thought back to the arrival of the gentleman from whom she distanced herself. To the lovely, intelligent Elizabeth Bennet, the two weeks of Mr. Collins' visit had felt more like two months. Her distant cousin, and the heir to her family home, Longbourn, was a bumbling, sycophantic fool. He had the ability to annoy her without even opening his mouth, and his officious attentions had become a drain on Elizabeth's spirits. She was a bright, happy, and kind young lady with a lively wit and bubbling sense of humor. The man's oppressive attentions weighed upon her.

Mr. Collins initially expressed interest in the eldest Bennet sister, but her mother was quick to turn the parson's interest to her second daughter. Elizabeth's eldest sister, Jane, the most beautiful and gentlest of all five Bennet sisters, was currently being courted by the newest resident of Meryton. Mr. Charles Bingley, a single young man of good fortune, had leased Netherfield Park, the Bennets' neighboring estate, shortly after Michaelmas. From the moment he laid eyes on Jane Bennet, Mr. Bingley had been utterly smitten. Unfortunately, the courtship existed only in Mrs. Bennet's mind, though Elizabeth believed it would be official in the very near future.

Upon first seeing him, Elizabeth thought Mr. Bingley's friend, Mr. Fitzwilliam Darcy of Pemberley in Derbyshire, to be very handsome.

However, Elizabeth overheard him decry her as not handsome enough to tempt him to dance. Since then, she had been unable to get Mr. Darcy out of her mind, though most of their interactions were more like verbal skirmishes than conversations. However, Mr. Darcy quite confused her. He often came across as proud and arrogant but also defended her when Mr. Bingley's shrew of a sister hurled thinly veiled insults at Elizabeth. Then again, there were his despicable actions against Mr. Wickham. The man was a conundrum Elizabeth could not decipher.

At present, it was not her disconcerting neighbor on her mind, but, rather, her dolt of a cousin. Elizabeth's mother, whose single goal in life was arranging marriages for her many daughters, pushed Elizabeth toward her cousin and Mr. Bennet's heir without considering how mismatched the two were. If Mrs. Bennet possessed more sense, she would have guided Mr. Collins in the direction of her middle daughter, Mary. Mary was quiet, studious, devout, and strictly upright. She and Mr. Collins made for a much better match.

Elizabeth lived in dread of Mr. Collins proposing. If he did, she would instantly refuse, which would infuriate Mrs. Bennet. Though Mr. Bennet agreed with Elizabeth's opinion of the utterly ridiculous parson, his second daughter doubted he possessed the fortitude to withstand her mother's endless complaints and attacks of nerves to support Elizabeth in her decision to not marry her father's heir.

Elizabeth sat lost in thought, wondering if there was anything she could do to prevent Mr. Collins from declaring his intentions. She gave her wit freedom when she responded to her cousin's ridiculous declarations and pontifications, but, unhappily for her, the man was too dense to understand her subtle insults. Moreover, though Mrs. Bennet might suspect Elizabeth's words, she did not possess the intelligence to take her meaning, either. With her mind a million miles away, Elizabeth failed to notice the approaching footfalls.

Since the plans for the ball began, Caroline Bingley had demanded Darcy's attention, saying that as their special guest she did not wish to make any decisions that did not meet with Mr. Darcy's desires and approval. So much time in close company with the clingy and demanding Miss Bingley had made Darcy desperate for fresh air and time away from her whining voice. Though he despised disguise of any sort, he claimed work that needed his attention. Then, Darcy snuck from the house through the kitchen and made his way to the stables with all haste. He tapped his foot impatiently while waiting for the groom to saddle his favorite horse, watching over his shoulder to ensure that Miss Bingley did not come upon him unawares. Once settled in the saddle, he kicked the beast into a gallop and rode away from Netherfield as fast as his mount could carry him.

As Darcy left the house behind, thoughts of the evening filled his head. He usually did not enjoy a ball, but tonight he anticipated finally dancing with Miss Elizabeth Bennet. Since observing Elizabeth Bennet at the Meryton Assembly and on multiple occasions since then, he had found that the young lady intrigued and drew him as no other woman ever had. What did it mean that she had refused his hand for a dance several times since they were introduced? *Could she have overheard my ridiculous comments to Bingley the night of the assembly and believe that I do not wish to dance with her?* Having never before experienced such rejection, Darcy rationalized that the room was too crowded or that she, indeed, needed to attend to her sisters or some other plausible excuse. With these thoughts, Darcy determined to ask Miss Elizabeth to dance the supper set so that she would recognize that he truly desired her company. That particular set would allow him to enjoy her sparkling personality for as long as possible. A moment of doubt assailed him. Would she turn him down yet again? Darcy determined to watch for the Bennets' arrival and present himself in the hallway when they entered. He would offer Miss Elizabeth an apology if she had overheard his harsh words and then would ask her to dance.

Darcy reached the base of a large hill. Having heard of Oakham Mount since arriving in the neighborhood, he decided to walk to the top to enjoy the view. After tying his mount to a low tree branch that would allow it to graze in his absence, he started the climb. When he reached the summit, he found the view before him to be more spectacular than expected. Miss Elizabeth Bennet sat on a rock, her knees drawn up to her chest, her chin resting upon them. Her bonnet sat beside her, and her face was turned away from him. Many of Elizabeth's dark curls cascaded down her back, having come loose from her coiffure during her rapid travels. The sun created a bright halo around her, bathing her in a golden glow.

"Miss Elizabeth, what a pleasant surprise."

The richness of the resonant voice behind her drew Elizabeth from her thoughts. Turning in surprise, she was briefly distracted by the handsome gentleman who often filled her thoughts. Darcy wore a dark green coat with buff breeches. The colors in his striped waistcoat matched the rest of his attire. His greatcoat swirled about him in the breeze while mud spattered his brown boots. Bright eyes, a dimpled smile, and two dark curly locks that fell over his brow completed his dashing appearance. In seconds, Elizabeth took all that in before crying in surprise, "Mr. Darcy, what are you doing here?"

A SURPRISE ENCOUNTER

"I APOLOGIZE FOR STARTLING YOU, MISS Elizabeth. Many of those whom I have met mentioned the outstanding view available from this point. I thought it would be best to enjoy some quiet and avoid the chaos at Netherfield as the final preparations for the ball take place." Looking out at the view, Darcy commented, "Its reputation is well-deserved."

"You are correct," agreed Elizabeth. "It is my favorite spot in all the area. I love that I can observe the entirety of my little corner of the world from here. It is often my refuge from the chaos of my home." Surprised at her candid reply, Elizabeth blushed.

"If I am not too presumptuous, from what did you need refuge today? I would have thought you and your sisters would be busy preparing for the ball tonight." Remembering his concerns about her possible poor opinion of him, he accompanied his words with a smile.

Surprised by his attempt at humor, Elizabeth answered more directly than she might have otherwise. "I needed to distance myself from Mr. Collins. I believe he plans to ask a question that I would prefer not to answer. If he cannot find me, he cannot ask."

Darcy wondered who Mr. Collins was. He vaguely recalled a homely little parson who had been with the Bennets when Darcy had last seen them in Meryton. "And who is Mr. Collins?"

"Mr. Collins is a distant cousin and the heir to my father's estate since it is entailed on the male line. He is visiting for a short time from his home in Hunsford, where he holds a living gifted to him by Lady Catherine de Bourgh. Mr. Collins praises the lady as if she were a deity, or perhaps a queen. However, from his descriptions, she sounds more like an autocratic busybody." Elizabeth wondered why she had added that last bit, but she felt somewhat addled by Mr. Darcy's sudden appearance. Elizabeth looked quite startled when Mr. Darcy laughed out loud at her words. "Mr. Darcy, are you well?" she could not help but ask, as she had never before heard laughter from the gentleman.

"I am quite well, Miss Elizabeth. I am impressed with your ability to so accurately judge another from just a few words. Though, if I am not mistaken, Mr. Collins probably spoke a great many words on the subject."

"You are correct, sir, but how did you know that? Have you met Mr. Collins previously?"

"No, but I do know my aunt very well and am familiar with the type of people she prefers around her."

"I am sorry, sir, but what has your aunt to do with anything?"

"Were you not aware that Lady Catherine de Bourgh is my aunt?"

Elizabeth's face flushed in embarrassment at her incautious words. "No, sir, I did not know. I apologize for speaking my opinion so freely. I did not mean to offend you." Elizabeth could not meet the gentleman's eyes, as she had given him another reason to disparage her.

"No apology is needed, Miss Elizabeth, for your analysis of my aunt's character was quite apt. She believes herself to be an authority on every subject and expects her words to be taken as gospel. Lady Catherine surrounds herself with weak individuals whom she can control and who will give her the constant praise she feels is her due."

Elizabeth's delightful laugh bubbled forth. "Well, that description certainly suits my cousin. In fact, it was your aunt's idea that he search for a wife among the cousins whom he will displace when he inherits their home. It is one idea I wish Lady Catherine had kept to herself." A huff of frustration accompanied her words.

"You are not the only person to wish she would keep her matrimonial ideas to herself. For years, my aunt has insisted that she and my mother agreed to my marrying Lady Catherine's daughter, Anne. My mother might have discussed such an idea once, but before her passing, she told me that I should follow my heart and marry only someone for whom I felt a deep and abiding love." Elizabeth was shocked to hear that a man of Mr. Darcy's station wanted to marry for love. "My cousin and I discussed the matter, and neither of us wishes to marry the other. We are both, by nature, shy and reserved. If we were to marry, Pemberley would be quiet as a tomb."

This conversation with Mr. Darcy was quite revealing, as he was contradicting many of Elizabeth's opinions of the gentleman. Could it be that his apparent pride was no more than shyness? She thought about their interaction at Netherfield Park during Jane's illness. Mr. Darcy had been quick to engage her in conversation then. Could he have been enjoying the wordplay and not serious in his declarations? He had even added a trait she possessed to Miss Bingley's list of skills an accomplished woman must have. Could there be more to the gentleman than met the eye? Could there also be more to the situation with Mr. Wickham? She decided to introduce his name into the conversation to learn more about their differences.

"There must be others who expect that you will marry your cousin. It was Mr. Wickham who mentioned the engagement to me." When she uttered that gentleman's name, Elizabeth saw Mr. Darcy's entire body stiffen. His fists clenched in anger. She scrutinized him cautiously, not knowing what he might do.

Taking a deep breath, Darcy turned to Elizabeth and said, "Miss Bennet, I know that you are an intelligent young woman, but I must caution you to not trust all of Mr. Wickham's words. He is a talented and experienced liar. His lies always contain a touch of the truth, which makes them more believable. However, he frequently uses his lies to manipulate other people for his own enjoyment. I would hate for you to become one of his victims."

Elizabeth was startled by Mr. Darcy's words. Did Mr. Wickham notice something in her reaction to the meeting between the two gentlemen and desire to turn her opinion further against Mr. Darcy? Ashamedly, Elizabeth realized she had not hesitated to spread Mr. Wickham's tale of woe. In fact, Wickham had said he would not speak against the younger Mr. Darcy as long as he held the elder one in esteem. Had Mr. Wickham manipulated Elizabeth into speaking for him? She was ashamed that she might have done just that and damaged Mr. Darcy's reputation without foundation.

"Mr. Darcy, Mr. Wickham told me a story about you that was most unflattering. Would you be willing to tell me your side of the situation?"

Darcy gave a slight nod of his head. The tension in his body was still present, and she realized that, with sheer determination, he was controlling the anger Wickham occasioned in him. "What tale did he tell you?" Elizabeth opened her mouth to speak, but before she could, Mr. Darcy continued. "No, wait. Let me guess. He gave you a sad story of my denying him a living that had been left to him in my father's will?" Elizabeth's sharply indrawn breath acknowledged the truth of his guess; she nodded in response. "My history with Mr. Wickham is a long one. Might I sit down before telling you the whole of it?"

"Of course, sir. Please forgive my rudeness for not offering sooner."

"Do not concern yourself, Miss Bennet," replied Darcy as he settled on the rock on which Elizabeth sat. "George Wickham is the son of my father's former steward. The elder Mr. Wickham was an excellent, honorable man. He had my father's trust and respect. Consequently, when Mr. Wickham asked my father to be godfather to his first child, my father agreed. The elder Mr. Wickham died when George was fifteen. In thanks for the man's years of dedicated work at Pemberley, Father sent George to university with me. The behavior George exhibited while we were at school and away from my father's watchful eye was disgusting. He devoted his time to drinking, gambling, and women. I am not sure he ever opened a book while at Cambridge. He received a gentleman's education and was left the living at Kympton in my father's will. However, a few weeks after my father's death, Wickham presented himself to me for his inheritance. When he learned what it was, he was angry. Based on his complaints, it was plain that Wickham expected that my father would leave him one of his estates. Wickham said he did not think himself suited to be a clergyman and requested the value of the living. After much negotiation, we settled on three thousand pounds." Again, Elizabeth emitted a gasp of surprise. "He received that plus the one thousand pounds my father left him. To protect myself, I had him sign away all rights to the living in exchange for the money.

"I told him our business was through, and I did not wish him to contact me ever again. Two years later, he returned, hat in hand and broke, and demanded the living that recently had become vacant. I reminded him of the papers he had signed and I refused to give him the position. There is more to my dislike for the man, but it is not my story to tell. I will only caution you to not allow yourself or your sisters to be alone with George Wickham, for he is not to be trusted where innocent women are concerned. He cares not if he ruins a servant, a shop girl, or a gently-born lady."

Elizabeth was horrified at the things she had learned from Mr. Darcy. She was also angry with herself for letting her prejudices blind her to the truth of the man's behavior. The signs that he was not truthful were there, but she either did not or chose not to see them. "I owe you an apology for allowing Mr. Wickham's words to influence my view of you, Mr. Darcy. It would appear I was angry with you for your words at the assembly and allowed that to color my thinking. Unfortunately, I also repeated his sad story, for which I am most heartily sorry."

"Oh, Miss Elizabeth, I am so sorry you heard that. I did not mean a word I said to Bingley. As I mentioned earlier, I am somewhat shy. Large crowds of unknown people make me uneasy. Add that to the rumors of my wealth and availability, and I was extremely uncomfortable. It is the same wherever I go. I detest being looked at like a prize bull at market." Elizabeth giggled at his expression. "Please accept my sincere apology for my disgraceful and dishonorable words. You are, in fact, the most handsome woman of my acquaintance."

Elizabeth looked doubtful at his words, but his eyes held nothing but sincerity. "Though I must question your eyesight, as you have seen my elder sister, I thank you for the compliment."

"It is no more than the truth," said Darcy firmly. "I am glad we had the opportunity to speak, Miss Elizabeth, for there is something I would like to ask you."

"And what might that be, Mr. Darcy?" asked Elizabeth archly, her brow raised questioningly.

"Might I request your first dance of the evening?"

"I should like very much to grant it to you, Mr. Darcy, but unfortunately, it has already been solicited by Mr. Collins. I tried to dissuade him, even suggesting that Lady Catherine would not find it appropriate, but he could not be swayed. Perhaps there is another set you might like." Elizabeth's obvious disappointment at not being able to accept filled Darcy with happiness.

"May I request the supper set, then?"

"I should be delighted to accept, sir. What shall we discuss this evening, do you think?"

"What is your opinion of books, Miss Bennet?"

"They are one of my favorite things, Mr. Darcy, but I fear I must say goodbye for now, or I will not be ready in time for the ball."

"Might I walk with you back to Longbourn?"

"If you wish to walk with me to the back garden wall, I would enjoy the company. I hope to sneak into the house via the kitchen to avoid Mr. Collins."

The two descended the hill to where Mr. Darcy's horse waited. He untied the horse, held the reins in his right hand, and offered his left arm to Elizabeth. They conversed as they walked, the topics wide-ranging.

As they neared their destination, Mr. Darcy said, "May I ask you an impertinent question, Miss Elizabeth?" Startled, she looked at him and gave a slight nod. "Is the question you are trying to avoid a proposal of marriage?"

Her face blushing brightly, Elizabeth nodded. "It is, sir. Mr. Collins and I are not at all suited to each other. I am afraid that if he were to propose, my mother might insist on the marriage. She fears being tossed into the hedgerows upon my father's death, especially if none of her daughters are yet wed."

"I can see where such concerns might greatly influence a mother's desires for her daughters. Would you be opposed to my attempting to dissuade him in his attention to you?"

"Not at all, but I wish you better luck than I had."

"This is where knowledge of my aunt might be used to good purpose."

Elizabeth laughed. "I tried to turn his attention to Mary, as I think she appreciates Mr. Collins. They have similar interests and Mary would be well suited to being a parson's wife."

"Then please allow me to see what I can do."

"I would appreciate any assistance you can provide. I find it hard to be polite to Mr. Collins after more than a few minutes in his company."

"Knowing my aunt's type, I can easily believe Mr. Collins might try the patience of a saint." Seeing the opening in the garden wall, Darcy said, "We have arrived, Miss Elizabeth." He took the hand resting on his arm and bowed over it, then placed the lightest of kisses on her knuckles. "Until this evening, Miss Elizabeth."

Elizabeth watched as he mounted his horse and turned in the direction of Netherfield. She opened the kitchen door a crack and listened before entering. Cook was stirring a pot on the stove and Mrs. Hill sat at the table with a cup of tea. She glanced up at Lizzy, a look of understanding in her eyes. Elizabeth spread her arms and shrugged her shoulders, causing the housekeeper to smile.

"Hurry up the back stairs, Miss Lizzy. I shall bring you some water and assist you myself."

"I appreciate that, Mrs. Hill, but I do not wish to be ready until we must walk out the door, if at all possible."

"I will assist you in any way I can."

"One thing you might do is ensure that Mary is looking her very best tonight. I am hoping to encourage Mr. Collins in her direction."

"After I bring your water, I will check on Miss Mary before returning to you."

"Thank you, Mrs. Hill. You are a wonder! What would I do without you?"

"Be in a great deal more trouble with your mother, I would imagine." Elizabeth laughed lightly as she bounded up the stairs. The housekeeper shook her head as she watched her favorite of the Bennets' daughters disappear from sight.

Elizabeth was the last of the family to enter the carriage, coming down only when her mother threatened to leave without her.

Mrs. Bennet stood in the doorway, waiting for Elizabeth. She grabbed her daughter's arm as Elizabeth attempted to exit. "I am very displeased with you, Lizzy. Mr. Collins particularly wished to walk with you today. It was very rude of you to run off and leave him. I demand that you give him your attention at the ball this evening. There will be consequences if you do not show him the proper respect." She turned and stalked towards the carriage without waiting for Elizabeth's reply

"Yes, Mama," said Elizabeth with a roll of her eyes, seen only by her father. Mr. Bennet handed Elizabeth into the carriage. Mr. Collins made to follow.

Mr. Bennet put out his arm to prevent the gentleman from entering. "It is far too crowded in the carriage for an unmarried man to be so close to my daughters. You will need to ride with the footman at the back. I will sit with the driver."

"You would force your guest to ride on your carriage like a servant?" demanded a nervous Mr. Collins. *I shall embarrass myself if I fall and look a fool in front of Cousin Elizabeth.*

"It is that, or you may walk, Mr. Collins. I will not allow you to sit in such close proximity to my daughters."

"Then I demand to sit with the driver."

"Mr. Collins you are nearly half my age. If anyone is to ride on the back, it is you. Alternatively, you may stay at Longbourn, if you prefer. Make your decision, Mr. Collins. It is time to leave." Mr. Bennet mounted to his seat beside the driver. Waiting for only a second, Mr. Collins scurried onto the back. He held on for dear life as the carriage moved forward.

AT CROSS PURPOSES

WHEN THE CARRIAGE PULLED TO A stop before the Netherfield steps to allow the passengers to disembark, Mr. Collins practically fell from it. He landed on his knees and appeared to kiss the ground. When he once again gained his feet, Lydia and Kitty could not contain their laughter. His greasy hair, which was usually combed to cover a bald spot, stood up straight, exposing his bare head. Sweat dripped from his face and his cravat was in disarray. Elizabeth and Jane ignored the man as they followed their parents towards the door. Once their laughter was under control, the younger girls followed their sisters. Only Mary waited for her cousin.

"I am sure there will be someplace where you can repair your attire once we have greeted our hosts," she said.

Extremely angry at the treatment by his cousins, Mr. Collins failed to offer Mary his arm as he stalked after the younger girls. A sad smile crossed Mary's face as she followed Mr. Collins.

Several people had joined the line of guests waiting to greet their hosts. Mr. Collins attempted to push his way forward to join his cousins, but a footman requested that he, please, maintain his place in the line. When he finally reached his host, Miss Bingley gazed at the parson as if he were a bug to squash underfoot. Mr. Collins rushed through the receiving line to find Cousin Elizabeth. He was disturbed to see her standing with Cousin Jane and a tall, handsome gentleman.

"Ah, Cousin Elizabeth, I beg your forgiveness for not escorting you inside as I should have."

"Jane and I were quite fine with my parents, sir. There was no need for you." Jane's elbow made discrete contact with Elizabeth's ribs at her rude statement. "To accompany us," she added belatedly.

"Miss Elizabeth, might you introduce me to this gentleman?"

"Mr. Fitzwilliam Darcy, this is Mr. William Collins, rector of Hunsford."

Looking at Elizabeth, Mr. Collins asked with excitement, "Mr. Darcy of Pemberley in Derbyshire?" She did not get the chance to nod in agreement before the gentleman launched into a long-winded speech. "How do you do, Mr. Darcy? I am honored to meet the nephew of my great patroness, your gracious aunt, Lady Catherine de Bourgh. It gives me great pleasure to tell you that your aunt and dear cousin were both in excellent health when I left them almost a fortnight ago."

Darcy rolled his eyes, causing a quickly-cut-off giggle to escape Elizabeth. "It appears you have had a mishap, Mr. Collins. Allow me to show you to the withdrawing room."

"Just like your aunt, you are all kindness and condescension. My thanks to you. . ." Mr. Collins' voice faded away. Elizabeth and Jane just stared after the gentlemen.

Darcy entered the gentlemen's withdrawing room behind the parson. He took advantage of his captive audience as the man began to address the deficiencies in his appearance. "I heard from my aunt that she sent you here to find a bride. I am sure she will be pleased with your choice of Miss Mary."

"Miss Mary. . .no, Mr. Darcy, you are mistaken. It is Cousin Elizabeth who is my choice."

"Miss Elizabeth? You surprise me, Mr. Collins. You must be quite brave to present such an outspoken woman to my aunt."

"Brave. . .ah. . .ah. . .outspoken? Cousin Elizabeth does seem to like to talk, but I am sure she will show the proper respect when presented to your distinguished aunt."

Mr. Darcy allowed a brief chuckle to escape. "As I said, you are quite brave. Unless, of course, you desire to leave your post at Hunsford. I wish you luck, sir, but if I might make a suggestion, you might wish to reconsider. The lovely, quiet, and demure Miss Mary is much more what my aunt is expecting."

"Lovely? Miss Mary?"

Darcy took offense at the disdain in the parson's voice. Miss Mary's loveliness might be more understated than some of her sisters, but your comment was very ungentlemanly, Lady Catherine would be most displeased to hear you disparaging such a proper young lady. *After what I said about Elizabeth at the Assembly, I should apologize again.* A gasp from Mr. Collins showed that he had caught the other meaning in Mr. Darcy's words. "Unhappy at Hunsford! Preposterous. No one could be unhappy in such a place and under the gracious auspices of your lady aunt."

"Oh, I thought perhaps with your bold choice, you were tired of your position and looking for another one."

"You think Lady Catherine would take Cousin Elizabeth in dislike?"

"I do not think she will take her in dislike except, perhaps, as her parson's wife."

"But whatever shall I do? I am to dance the first set with Cousin Elizabeth."

"It is only a dance."

"But the lady is expecting my proposal. If I dance with her, it shall only set her up for heartbreak."

Darcy bowed his head to hide the astonishment and disbelief in his expression. "Well, if it would be of assistance, I suppose I could take her off your hands for the first dance. I can let her down gently for you."

"Just like your aunt, your are all that is good, Mr. Darcy. It is no wonder you are related to my magnanimous patroness."

"Well, please excuse me, I must find Miss Elizabeth and explain before the first set begins. You must hurry if you wish to find Miss Mary before another partner claims her."

As Darcy entered the ballroom, he smiled widely. His eyes searched the room for Elizabeth. As such, he did not notice Miss Bingley until she grasped hold of his arm. "There you are, Mr. Darcy. I was looking for a partner with whom to open the evening. You would be perfect."

Peeling Miss Bingley's hand from his arm, Darcy said, "I am sorry, but I already have a partner for the first set." He gave her the briefest nod of his head before walking away. She stared after him with a look of frustration.

Watching from across the room, Elizabeth wondered at Miss Bingley's boldness in grabbing Darcy's arm so, but he quickly disentangled himself from her and made his way to Elizabeth's side with a handsome smile upon his face.

"Miss Elizabeth, Mr. Collins asked that I offer you his deepest regrets. He forgot that he had promised the first dance to Miss Mary. Might I offer myself as a substitute?"

"You are all kindness, Mr. Darcy. Thank you for offering to take Mr. Collins' place rather than requiring that I sit out. I would be pleased to accept your generous offer." Darcy put out his hand to lead her to the floor as Bingley approached to collect Jane.

When Mr. Bingley reached her side, Jane was staring after the departing couple, a confused expression on her face. "Miss Bennet," he said, offering her his hand. He then caught her expression. "Is everything all right?"

Jane turned and gave him a bright smile. "No, there is nothing wrong. I am just bemused at the exchange I observed between Lizzy and Mr. Darcy. Their banter was quite friendly and bordered on flirting."

"Flirting? Darcy and Miss Elizabeth? That is a situation which bears watching. . .when I can spare the attention from my lovely partner." Bingley stared deeply into the blue eyes of the beauty standing before him. A flush covered her face. Jane's smile grew as she accompanied Mr. Bingley to their place in the set that was forming.

Darcy and Elizabeth took the third place in the set, with Mr. Hurst between Darcy and Bingley. From the corner of his eye, Darcy noticed Mrs. Hurst's forehead pucker, while from behind Elizabeth's back, Miss Bingley glared at him before turning away, her nose tilted in the air. With the harsh look on her face, none of the local gentlemen dared approach her to ask for a dance. Darcy did not care; he was delighted with his partner and smiled brightly at Elizabeth. Her answering smile made his heart rejoice. They moved through the opening steps of the dance without speaking but never taking their eyes off of one another.

Elizabeth was the first to speak. "We talked this morning of discussing books while we danced. First, would you please tell me of your conversation with Mr. Collins?"

A chuckle met her question. When Darcy had his humor under control, he complied with her request, relating the entire conversation to Elizabeth.

Her bubbling laugh was like music to his ears. "What a ridiculous man! To believe that I—or any woman, for that matter—would be heartbroken over such a pompous buffoon."

"I cannot argue with your assessment of the gentleman." Mr. Darcy's smile showed his dimples. "Since you will be missing the attention of your suitor, might you allow me to occupy some of your time? I should like very much to become better acquainted."

"I would like that as well, Mr. Darcy. Shall we discuss books now, sir?" Elizabeth's arch look and bright smile brought forth Mr. Darcy's dimples.

"Whatever you wish, Miss Elizabeth.

They discussed their favorites in literature, which of Shakespeare's plays they preferred, and their favorite poets. Both were surprised to find that their tastes were quite similar. At the conclusion of the dance, they joined Jane and Bingley to visit while waiting for the next set. Before anyone else approached the ladies to request a dance, Darcy asked Jane for the second set and Bingley asked Elizabeth. They stood together talking as they waited for the music to begin, then walked onto the floor and took places in the set beside one another. As they danced, Darcy questioned Jane about Elizabeth's interests and preferences. The conversation between the other couple was equally informative to Elizabeth.

"What did you do to Darcy, Miss Elizabeth? I have never seen him so happy to dance before."

"Whatever do you mean, Mr. Bingley?"

"Darcy is constantly sought after by women–including my sister–who wish to capture him for his name and fortune. Consequently, he never dances the first set, as he does not wish to show favoritism to any young woman. Darcy also does not dance twice with any young lady. He surprised me tonight by dancing the first set and allowing his pleasure to show. He usually wears what some of us affectionately refer to as the Darcy mask. He is quite adept at hiding his emotions, but those of us who know him well–or, should I say, understand him well–know him to be kind, generous, and extremely protective of those for whom he cares."

"I have seen how serious Mr. Darcy can be. Perhaps he will let me see this other side you mentioned."

"Well, enough about Darcy. Can you tell me a few of Miss Jane's favorite things?"

"What would you like to know?"

By the time the second set concluded, the gentlemen both felt that they knew their respective ladies a little better.

After dancing the first two sets, Darcy watched as Elizabeth danced with another gentleman. He was surprised at the feeling of jealousy that washed over him to see Elizabeth in the arms of another man. Darcy danced the fourth set with Elizabeth's dearest friend, Charlotte Lucas, from whom he learned even more about Miss Elizabeth. When they finished, he walked to where Elizabeth stood with Jane and Bingley. Darcy opened his mouth to ask Elizabeth how she had enjoyed her last two sets, but Miss Bingley arrived and attached herself to his arm.

"You did not forget that you promised me the supper set, did you, Mr. Darcy?"

Darcy removed her from his arm. In a clipped tone, he said, "I believe you are mistaken, Miss Bingley. I asked you for the eighth set, as I already have a partner for the supper set." Stepping away, he offered his hand to Elizabeth and led her to the floor to join the set currently forming.

Miss Bingley stood there with her mouth gaping. First, he had danced the opening set, and now the supper set, with that dreadful upstart Eliza Bennet. She depended on having his company for dinner. Now she would have to sit alone with Louisa and Hurst, as she had no partner. How could this be happening to her? Caroline stalked from the ballroom and into the dining room, where she barked at a servant or two to release her anger.

As they walked onto the floor, Elizabeth whispered, "Did you forget you asked Miss Bingley to dance?"

"Not at all. I leave before the supper set at most balls. I assume Miss Bingley felt she might force my hand."

"Are all of the ladies of your acquaintance so aggressive?"

"Unfortunately, the majority of them are."

Elizabeth laughed lightly. "Poor Mr. Darcy. How hard it must be to be so in demand."

"How unkind of you to laugh at me. Even though I do not particularly care for balls, there are several that I am required to attend. Having to protect myself from predatory women takes away any pleasure I might derive from the event."

"I am sorry, Mr. Darcy. It was unkind of me to tease in this instance. I suppose I find the ridiculous behavior of women like Miss Bingley amusing. I doubt I would feel that way were I in your shoes."

"I must say, dancing with you tonight has made this the most enjoyable ball I have ever attended." Darcy held her gaze as he spoke, causing a beautiful rose pink blush to cover Elizabeth's face.

Flattered by his words, Elizabeth found herself in the unusual position of being speechless. Since words failed her, she stared back, a shy smile of pleasure on her face. They finished the dance in silence, but their eyes spoke volumes.

When the set was over, they found Bingley and Jane, then moved together into the dining room. The two couples sat at the head table along with the Hursts. Caroline was about to take a seat when Mr. Collins stepped past her and seated Mary, then took the last place at the table, beside Mr. Darcy.

Bingley stood. "I would like to welcome you all to Netherfield tonight. My dear friends and neighbors, you have made my family and me most welcome in our new home. I hope that you will enjoy yourselves tonight."

When Bingley took his seat, dozens of liveried servants began to serve the white soup. Each time Darcy began to speak to Elizabeth, Mr. Collins interrupted him with a comment about his aunt.

Darcy let out a huff and ground his teeth before turning to the gentleman on his left. "Mr. Collins, your time would be better spent getting to know the companion of your future life, as I believe you termed it. If this were a regular dinner party, you would converse with both your dinner partners. However, the supper set at a ball is designed to allow you to know your partner better."

"I appreciate your advice, sir. However, I must keep Miss Elizabeth from attracting you because of your betrothal to Miss de Bourgh. Your aunt would not forgive me if my cousin were to entrap you and keep you from your duty."

"I believe I am quite capable of managing Miss Elizabeth without your advice, Mr. Collins." Darcy's tone was as arrogant as any ever heard from Lady Catherine de Bourgh."

"My apologies, sir. However, I shall devote myself to Miss Mary and still do my duty to keep my cousin from attaching herself to you too often."

With a glare, Darcy turned back to Elizabeth. He opened his mouth to speak, but at her unhappy expression, he paused. "Is something the matter, Miss Elizabeth?"

In a clipped, cold voice, Elizabeth answered without looking at the gentleman. "I thought better of you, sir. Please explain why, if you are betrothed, you would desire to know me better."

Darcy was affronted that she would doubt his honor, but he realized that he was still earning her trust. "I told you of my aunt's desires as well as those of my cousin, Anne and I."

"Why would your aunt speak of an engagement when none exists?" Elizabeth relaxed her posture and spoke less harshly. "Is she attempting to force your hand? Will you be required to marry Miss de Bourgh?"

"Lady Catherine speaks of the engagement to everyone in the family. With what you have learned of her, are you surprised that she would speak of her desires to her clergyman, especially one who agrees with her every wish?"

Elizabeth looked at him. "Your heart is your own to give where you choose."

"I am afraid not." Elizabeth's expression grew cold again, so Darcy hurriedly continued. "For it already belongs to you." Elizabeth's mouth formed an "o" as that same sound gushed forth on a whisper. "I did not mean to announce it so soon. I hoped that I might court you properly and win your affections."

"I am not averse to that idea, sir." Elizabeth's posture and expression spoke of her pleasure at his pronouncements. "But what if your aunt should learn of your plans? Is there anything she can do that will change your mind?"

"The only thing that will change my mind would be if you should decide against me. Even then, I doubt that I could ever love another. You are the first young lady to ever draw my interest. I believe you are my other half, the only person who can complete my life."

Elizabeth was astounded by the words from the quiet man from Derbyshire. "After our talk earlier, I was ready to admit my original attraction. I would very much like the opportunity to see what might develop between us, Mr. Darcy." Her words to this point had been softly spoken, but when she caught Mr. Collins leaning in to overhear their conversation, she gently touched Mr. Darcy's arm.

His glare again in place, he turned to the parson. "Why are you invading my personal space, Mr. Collins?"

Instead of leaning away, Collins leaned in closer, offering, "I thought you might need my help with Cousin Elizabeth. She can be rudely outspoken, and I would not hesitate to remind her of her place compared to yours."

"I will say it once more, Mr. Collins. I am perfectly capable of dealing with Miss Elizabeth without any assistance."

"Of course, Mr. Darcy. I am sure you are more than capable, just as your estimable aunt is."

"Then, as I suggested earlier, you should focus your attention on Miss Mary. If you do not woo her as she deserves, she may not accept an offer of marriage. Then you will have failed to comply with my aunt's instructions to you."

"Thank you so much for your concern and reminder, sir. I shall certainly attend to your words. I would never wish to disappoint my esteemed patroness."

When the dinner ended, Mr. Darcy escorted Miss Elizabeth back to the ballroom. He watched as she danced with her neighbor, Samuel Long. His next set was with Mrs. Hurst and then Miss Bingley. Darcy would have liked to have finished the night by dancing the final set with Elizabeth, but as they were not engaged, it would not be possible. Darcy would attend from the sidelines as Elizabeth danced, or he would talk with Elizabeth if she were not dancing.

The set with Mrs. Hurst was barely tolerable, as Darcy found her choice of conversation challenging.

"What do you think of Caroline's arrangements for the ball, Mr. Darcy? I believe that it would be acceptable even in the first circles, would it not?

"Everything is fine." Knowing what Mrs. Hurst was about, Darcy kept his answers as impersonal as possible.

"Caroline's menu was very diverse and quite above what anyone in this little town could expect."

"Yes, Charles is fortunate in the cook who came with the estate."

Louisa Hurst was frustrated that the gentleman did not say anything complimentary that she could repeat to Caroline.

"Does not Caroline shine in her gown? It is definitely more stylish than anything else displayed tonight."

"I am afraid that I prefer a more understated style. My dear mother always said elegance is found in simplicity."

Confounded by the gentleman's answers, Mrs. Hurst remained silent for the remainder of the dance.

Darcy returned the lady to her husband and found Miss Bingley waiting for him. While keeping his back to Miss Bingley, Darcy moved to speak to Bingley, who stood with the two eldest Bennet sisters.

"Who is your partner for this set, Miss Elizabeth?" asked Darcy.

"I am free this set. It shall be my turn to watch you from the sideline," replied Elizabeth with a laugh.

"I hope my performance will not disappoint." Smiling, he added, "I also pray you will forgive me if my conversation with my partner is somewhat lacking."

Over Mr. Darcy's shoulder, Elizabeth could see Miss Bingley watching them with a glare. "I believe there is a time for reticence, Mr. Darcy. If you think now is the time, I will happily agree."

As the music began for the next dance, Darcy smiled at Elizabeth, then went to retrieve his partner. He caught a glimpse of Miss Bingley's glare as he turned. Looking back at Elizabeth, he rolled his eyes and received a saucy grin in response. Elizabeth saw Darcy bow to Miss Bingley and offer his hand to lead her to the floor. She did not miss his flinch when the lady clutched his hand. Darcy kept his elbow stiff so that she could not draw closer to his side. Jane's partner came to solicit her hand, and Mr. Bingley excused himself to see to his duties as host.

A DANGEROUS ENCOUNTER

ELIZABETH WAS WATCHING MR. DARCY AND failed to hear her cousin approach. "Cousin Elizabeth."

"Mr. Collins, you startled me, sir. Where is Mary? You did not leave her unattended, did you?"

"I said that I would fetch her some punch."

"Then what are you doing here? Do you need directions to the dining room? You should fetch the punch and return to my sister." Not wishing to engage the gentleman, she turned back to her observation of the dancers.

"I will fetch the punch and return to Cousin Mary very soon. However, I feel it is my responsibility to caution you to be more circumspect in your dealings with Mr. Darcy. The gentleman is far above you in society and is promised to someone else."

"I don't believe my interactions with Mr. Darcy are any of your concern. I suggest that you return to your companion, sir." Elizabeth's cold tone and glare had no effect on the dense parson. When he opened his mouth to speak again, Elizabeth offered a brusque, "Excuse me," before walking away. She made for the doors to the balcony, where she could recover from her anger without the eyes of everyone in the ballroom on her.

Elizabeth leaned against the cold stone railing and took several deep breaths. She began to calm, but then an unexpected, and unwanted, voice came out of the darkness, causing her startled heart to race.

"Miss Elizabeth, how pleased I am to find you unattended. I hope that you have saved me a dance."

"Mr. Wickham, what are you doing here?"

"Did I not promise to dance with you at this ball? A gentleman must keep his promises." Wickham gave her a dashing smile while trying to hide his thrill at finding her unattended on the shadowy terrace. Perhaps he could accomplish more than a dance and ruin her, preventing Darcy from getting what he wished. "I did not seek to cause a disturbance at Mr. Bingley's ball, with the disagreeable Mr. Darcy in attendance. I have been watching for him to retire or for an opportunity to slip in for a dance. How fortunate that you needed a breath of fresh air and gave me the opportunity to fulfill my promise."

"I understood that Colonel Forster had you on guard duty this evening. How did you get away? I assume you are not derelict in your duties." Elizabeth intentionally infused archness into her tone,

Thinking quickly, Wickham said, "No, no, that is merely the story my friends are saying to put Darcy off. Now, about that dance. . ."

Elizabeth was quick to interrupt. "Mr. Wickham, it would hardly be appropriate for us to dance alone here on the balcony. If you are not willing to attend, I release you from your promise." Elizabeth attempted to keep her tone light, but her eyes said something entirely different.

Not being able to see her expression clearly in the dark, Wickham said, "Willingness has nothing to do with it, Miss Elizabeth. There is very little I would not be willing to do for you." *Or to you, for that matter.*

"How kind of you, Mr. Wickham. However, I must return inside." Keeping her cool, Elizabeth turned to reenter the house. She was prevented from doing so by his fingers clasping firmly around her wrist.

"You would not deny me the joy of dancing with you, would you, dear Miss Elizabeth?"

"I am afraid that I must, sir. The actions you are requesting that I take would put my reputation in jeopardy."

He tightened his grip and pulled her farther into the darkness. "I would never do anything to damage the reputation of such a fine lady. Here in the shadows at the far edge of the terrace, no one will be the wiser and your reputation will remain secure."

"I thank you for the offer, Mr. Wickham, but I did not bring my wrap and would prefer to return to the ballroom."

Wickham began rubbing circles on the back of her hand as he stepped closer. "I thought that we were friends, Miss Elizabeth." She looked back steadily but did not answer. After having learned so much about the man, Elizabeth was trying to subdue the fear that was beginning to snake along her spine.

"We are, sir, and as you are a friend and a gentleman, I ask you to release my arm and let me return to the ballroom before someone notices my absence."

Instead of complying with her request, Wickham stepped closer. "How can you deny a lonely soldier the comfort and enjoyment of a dance with such a lovely woman?"

"As I said before, I would be happy to dance when next we meet. Alternatively, if you care to enter through the front door, we could dance as planned in the ballroom. The decision is yours, Mr. Wickham, but no matter what you decide, I am returning to the ballroom now."

"Well, as you do not wish to dance now, and I do not wish to embarrass Mr. Bingley should his friend choose to cause a scene, you must offer me a gift in exchange for my disappointment."

"Now you are being silly, Mr. Wickham. I have nothing with me to give you as a gift, even if such a thing were appropriate, which it is not."

"You surprise me, Miss Elizabeth, I did not suspect you to be the type who was a stickler for the rules and conventions of society."

"Then you do not understand me as well as you think, sir. Moreover, based on your words and behavior, perhaps you are not the gentleman I thought you were. Now please release me and allow me to return inside."

Anger in his tone, Wickham cried, "I am a gentleman. I am more of a gentleman than that dull Darcy will ever be. I see you, like all the other women I've ever met, are willing to overlook his poor behavior for his money. I thought better of you. I thought I had finally found someone who saw Darcy for the scoundrel he is."

"I care nothing for Mr. Darcy's money. Character is what I value in a gentleman. He will have to earn my respect, and you are rapidly losing it, sir."

Wickham tightened his grip on Elizabeth's wrist and yanked her against his chest, twisting her arm behind her.

"Unhand me, you scoundrel. Now I know that Mr. Darcy told me the truth of your past with him. You are despicable, sir."

"Well, well, Darcy opened up to you. His attraction to you is stronger than I guessed. Did he tell you about his ruined little sister?

This must be the story Darcy said was not his to tell. I pray he is lying and Miss Darcy was not hurt. With all the defiance and disdain she could muster, Elizabeth retorted, "You are a liar, Mr. Wickham. Why should I believe anything you say? Now let me go."

"I do not think I will. I enjoy preventing Darcy from finding happiness. He may want you now, but I doubt his desire will remain when I am through with you."

With a sneer on his lips, his head descended towards Elizabeth, intent upon forcing a kiss. Unable to move her arm in its current position, she twisted her head to prevent him from capturing her lips. Not knowing what else she might do to avoid his assault, Lizzy closed her eyes, not wishing to observe this miserable first kiss experience. However, the attack she expected did not come. There was a painful tug on her arm before it was released. She bent it across her waist, rubbing the shoulder, and was surprised to discover Mr. Wickham laid out on the ground. Mr. Darcy rushed for her.

Without thinking, Darcy pulled her into his embrace. "You are safe now, Miss Elizabeth. Are you well? Did he hurt you?"

Darcy had let Caroline Bingley's incessant chatter wash over him. Could the woman never be silent? Her flirting and the fluttering of her lashes had turned his stomach. Whenever the dance had turned him in Elizabeth's direction, he would catch her eye and smile. However, when he had next turned, Mr. Collins had stood beside her. Elizabeth's flushed face and tense jaw, as well as the anger sparking in her eyes, had made it impossible to look away.

"What is that buffoon doing?"

Darcy's muttered words had reached his partner. "What did you say, Mr. Darcy?" Caroline had received no response to her question, so she had turned to follow his gaze. "Ahh, Miss Eliza is talking with her betrothed. At least, I heard Mrs. Bennet proclaiming that a betrothal would be forthcoming. How lucky for Miss Elizabeth. An arranged marriage is certainly the best to which that country nobody can aspire." Caroline's brittle laugh had followed her words.

Watching as an angry-looking Elizabeth rushed from the ballroom and onto the terrace, Darcy had turned to his companion and delivered a long-overdue setdown. "Actually, being a gentleman's daughter, Miss Elizabeth can aspire to just about any match, unlike you, as the daughter of a tradesman. You really should learn to be kinder to those above you in society if you wish to advance, Miss Bingley. Insulting your betters will get you nowhere." As the first dance in the set ended, Darcy had bowed and moved to follow Elizabeth. Her mouth agape, a shocked Caroline had just stared after the gentleman. When the music for the second dance had begun, she had looked around, her face embarrassed, and then rushed off to speak with a servant to cover the fact that her partner had abandoned her on the dance floor.

Darcy had tried to make his way around the ballroom to reach the doors to the terrace. Several of the single young ladies not currently dancing had attempted to place themselves in his path, hoping to gain his notice. He had only nodded at each as he continued on his way. When he had reached the door, he had seen that Elizabeth stood trapped against the balustrade with a gentleman attempting to take liberties. Darcy had grabbed the man's shoulder and spun him around. Upon seeing the person he most despised, Darcy had pulled back his arm and punched Wickham in the face with the full force of his anger, sending the man sprawling.

Elizabeth looked at Darcy in surprise for just a moment before realizing the comfort and safety she felt at being held in his arms. "I am well, Mr. Darcy. You arrived just in time to prevent anything serious from happening."

Darcy released her and stepped back, causing her a moment of disappointment at the loss of the warmth of his embrace. Not noticing the way Elizabeth cradled her arm, Darcy clamped his hand on Elizabeth's shoulder and pushed her to arm's length so that he could look into her eyes and check her for any injuries. As the pressure of his hand came down on her shoulder, Elizabeth flinched. "You are hurt! What did that scoundrel do to you?"

"It was nothing more than words until I tried to leave. Then Wickham twisted my hand behind me to prevent me from moving. You saw what he attempted next. Oh, thank you for arriving when you did."

"I am sorry I did not arrive in time to prevent you from being hurt. I will take you to the library. Then I can fetch your father and Mr. Jones."

"I do not wish to cause a scene at the ball. I will refrain from dancing and request that they call Mr. Jones after my walk tomorrow. My family will not find it surprising if I take a tumble while I walk."

"But you are in pain. You cannot go for so many hours in such discomfort. There must be something I can do to be of assistance?"

Elizabeth appreciated Mr. Darcy's solicitousness, so she asked, "Do you know if Mr. Bingley's housekeeper might have any willow bark? That can be brewed into a tea and would help with the pain."

"Let me take you to the library. I will arrange for the tea." Elizabeth accepted his offered arm and they started for the library. She paused and looked back." What are we going to do about Mr. Wickham? You cannot just leave him here. Perhaps before you escort me anywhere, you should collect Colonel Forster. I believe Mr. Wickham was on guard duty tonight. Perhaps he can be detained on dereliction of duty."

Darcy smiled widely. "What an excellent idea, Miss Elizabeth. Do you feel up to fetching the colonel? I would not wish to leave you here with this scoundrel, in case he should awaken."

Elizabeth nodded and stepped through the doors into the ballroom. Fortunately, the colonel was nearby, at the punch table. Elizabeth walked and whispered something to him. As the colonel moved onto the balcony, Elizabeth paused to request a glass of punch before following him.

Taking the glass with her, Elizabeth returned to the gentlemen on the balcony. Seeing the glass, Darcy took it from her and threw the liquid into Wickham's face. With a splutter, the man returned to consciousness. Jumping to his feet, Wickham cried, "What the devil, Darcy! Were you jealous that the woman you desire wanted me and not you?"

"Shut your mouth, Wickham." The menace in Darcy's voice was unmistakable.

"Lieutenant Wickham," said a sharp, commanding voice.

Wickham whirled to see his commanding officer standing before him. With a sharp salute, Wickham stood at attention.

"I distinctly remember assigning you guard duty this evening, Lieutenant. Would you like to explain your presence here?"

"I was sent with a message for you, Colonel."

"If that is the case, why are you here on the balcony? Why did you not enter through the front door to seek me?"

"I, uh, I thought I could be more discreet if I observed you from here, sir."

"Where is the message, Lieutenant?"

Wickham patted his pockets. "I, uh, it seems to have dropped from my pocket, sir."

"A likely story." Colonel Forster turned towards the ballroom and waved at two officers standing just inside the door. "Gentlemen, I am sorry to curtail your evening. However, Lieutenant Wickham is derelict in his duty. He abandoned his post of guard duty to sneak into the ball. Obtain some rope with which to bind him and then escort him to the brig. Once there, change his ropes for irons. He is to be guarded at all times and not by anyone in his command or those who are his close friends."

"Colonel, might I also suggest that you check into any debts Wickham has incurred while in the area," Darcy said. "He has a habit of running up debts and then running out of them. That would put the militia in a bad light."

"You will pay for this, Darcy. I will get my revenge."

"Who will believe you when they discover you deserted your post and then find out about your debts?"

"This is not over, Darcy."

"I believe it is. If the militia releases you, you will find yourself in debtor's prison. I have been buying up your debts ever since Cambridge. I have accumulated enough to keep you there until you are old and gray. If you survive that long."

OTHER ANNOYANCES

DARCY AND ELIZABETH WATCHED WICKHAM BEING dragged off, his curses echoing in the night air. When the militiamen were out of sight, Darcy put his arm around Elizabeth and guided her farther down the balcony to where the French doors led into the library. He helped her into a seat and was bowing over her hand when a loud voice screeched from the doorway.

"Cousin Elizabeth, how dare you attempt to compromise Mr. Darcy. I have already told you that he is betrothed to his cousin."

Darcy and Elizabeth looked at the door. There stood not only Mr. Collins but Mrs. Bennet and Mrs. Philips, their eyes wide and their mouths hanging open.

"Mr. Darcy, you have compromised my Lizzy. Now you will have to marry her!"

Mrs. Philips did not remain to learn anything further before rushing off to the ballroom to spread the gossip. Encountering Mr. Bennet first, she delightedly repeated the news to him in one long breath. Upon hearing what she had to say, Mr. Bennet paled slightly before escorting Mrs. Philips to her husband and demanding that he keep her quiet to protect the family's reputation. Then he hurried to the library. He reached the door in time to hear Mrs. Bennet berating his daughter.

Mr. Collins turned to his cousin's wife. "I am sorry, Mrs. Bennet, but Mr. Darcy is not free to marry Cousin Elizabeth. He is already betrothed."

"I do not care about a previous betrothal. Mr. Darcy has compromised my Lizzy, so they must marry."

"Mama, please keep your voice down. Mr. Darcy did not compromise me. He offered his assistance because I managed to hurt my arm. Mr. Darcy brought me here to rest. He planned to fetch Papa and Mr. Jones, as well as request some willow bark tea for me."

"Will you never learn to act like a lady, Lizzy? How did you manage to hurt your arm at a ball?"

"That is enough, Mrs. Bennet. You should be more concerned about Lizzy's injury than making ridiculous assumptions about a compromise."

"There is no compromise," stated Mr. Collins again. "Mr. Darcy is already—"

Mr. Darcy's cold voice abruptly cut off the parson. "Mr. Collins, I advise you to worry about your own affairs rather than assuming you know anything about mine."

"But Mr. Darcy, you cannot mean to go against your aunt's wishes. You are set to marry one of the greatest flowers of the kingdom."

"That is enough, Mr. Collins. I suggest you return to Miss Mary. You have ignored her far too long and risk disappointing my aunt. I will also remind you that despite what my aunt may say, you are not an intimate of mine, nor are you aware of my desires for my future. I will ask that you keep your opinions to yourself. Any mention you make of what you observed would definitely compromise Miss Elizabeth. Do not create a situation that might cause upset to my aunt or result in my having to challenge you." Mr. Collins would never do anything that might upset his patroness, nor would he wish to face the fearsome gentlemen before him on the field of honor.

As Mr. Collins turned to exit, he whispered to Mr. Bennet, "I trust that you will not take advantage of my absence to secure an advantageous match for your daughter."

"You can be assured that I will do what is best for everyone." Mr. Bennet watched his cousin return to the ballroom. Then, entering the library, he looked at his favorite daughter. "Lizzy, what is it that you need for your injury?"

"Just some willow bark tea, Papa."

Turning to his wife, he said, "Mrs. Bennet, please find Mr. Bingley and ask him to request the needed tea for Lizzy and send it here. Then please return to the ballroom and watch over our two youngest daughters. I believe they may both have imbibed too much punch and will soon embarrass the family." The elder lady turned to comply with his word, but stopped when he spoke again. "Also, Mrs. Bennet, if you mention one word of what you saw or heard, I will withhold your pin money for at least six months. Do I make myself clear?" Her eyes wide, Mrs. Bennet nodded and rushed from the room to locate Mr. Bingley.

Darcy took note of his words. *Bingley might find that a useful threat for controlling his sister.*

After his wife departed, Mr. Bennet closed the door and looked at the two young people remaining. "Now, would someone like to tell me what happened this evening?"

"It is nothing, Papa. I just managed to injure my shoulder–"

Mr. Darcy spoke at the same moment. "I was fortunate enough to come upon Miss Elizabeth in a moment of need, sir."

Eyebrows raised, Mr. Bennet asked, "And just what did she need?"

"I planned to speak to you on the morrow about a man in the neighborhood who presents a danger to your daughters. This so-called gentleman was forcing his attention on Miss Elizabeth when I arrived on the terrace. After subduing the gentleman, a member of the militia, I turned him over to his superior officer. Then I brought Miss Elizabeth here so that she could get the attention she needed."

"And just which officer was bothering my daughter?"

"Mr. Wickham."

"The same Mr. Wickham to whom you denied a living?"

"That is the story Wickham tells wherever he goes to gain sympathy and garner support. However, it is not the truth."

"And why should I believe you rather than accept Mr. Wickham's version of the events?"

Darcy was insulted that the gentleman would doubt his honor but attempted to maintain his composure. "The difference, sir, is that I can prove my story. My father did leave Wickham one thousand pounds and a living in his will. Wickham had no desire to be a clergyman, which was a great relief to me. The man I observed at school was not the type who should be in charge of the spirituality and well-being of anyone, much less an entire parish. He demanded money instead of the living. I gave him an additional three thousand pounds and he signed away all rights to the living. If you need to see the documents, I can send to my solicitor for them."

"That will not be necessary, as I believe you are telling the truth. However, I needed to know why I should trust you."

"I understand, sir. My natural reserve has not given the inhabitants of Meryton a reason to think well of me. As I mentioned, I planned to visit tomorrow to discuss the risk Wickham poses to your daughters. When Colonel Forster took him away, I suggested that he look into any debts that Wickham may have incurred. If he cannot pay them, I will cover them and add them to those I previously purchased. Though there is a risk that my actions could damage my family, putting him in debtor's prison seems the best choice rather than continuing to allow him to wreak havoc wherever he goes and abuse my name and my family's reputation."

"Just what, exactly, did Mr. Wickham do to you, Lizzy?"

Elizabeth blushed and looked down. "After a conversation with the annoying Mr. Collins, I excused myself to the terrace to cool down a bit. Mr. Wickham's voice came out of the darkness, startling me. He attempted to convince me to dance with him, but I refused to do so unless we were in the ballroom with the other guests. When I tried to return inside, he grabbed my arm and twisted it up behind me. Then he attempted to kiss me. Had Mr. Darcy not arrived when he did, Mr. Wickham might have attempted even more, at least if he followed through on his threats." Her face scarlet with embarrassment, Elizabeth would not meet her father's eyes. It was perhaps fortunate that her gaze remained lowered so that she could not see the anger building on Darcy's face.

Before anything further could be said, a knock came on the library door. The housekeeper appeared with the willow bark tea, followed by Jane and Bingley.

"Lizzy, are you well?"

"Miss Elizabeth, I am sorry you were hurt in my home. Is there anything I can do?"

"How did you know something was wrong?" she asked, worry evident in Elizabeth's voice.

"I was with Mr. Bingley when Mama came and said you needed willow bark tea. You hate the taste of that and use it only when you cannot bear the pain of some injury."

"Just a simple mishap. There is no cause for concern."

"Should I find Mr. Jones to ensure it is nothing serious?"

"I would prefer to wait until tomorrow. If it is still bothering me, we can send for Mr. Jones at that time."

In the ballroom, Miss Bingley looked about for Darcy and her brother, but they were nowhere in sight, nor could she find either of the eldest Bennet sisters. To Caroline Bingley, this was cause for great concern. *Could they possibly have slipped away to propose to those unsuitable Bennet women? I must find them. I must stop them before it is too late.* As she searched the room, a snippet of conversation caught her ear. "What were they doing in the library together?"

"I'm not sure, but–"

"That is enough, ladies. There is nothing to discuss until we understand all the circumstances." Mr. Philips' voice was low and adamant. A firm glare accompanied his words.

Those words struck terror into Caroline's heart, particularly considering whom she had overheard. Sneaking into the back hallway, Caroline entered the servants' passage. Then she quietly entered the library, not latching the wall tightly for fear the click would attract someone's attention. Bending over to avoid being seen, she snuck into a tall wingback chair facing the fireplace. Once she was sure no one had observed her entrance, Miss Bingley stood and spoke in a harsh, sneering voice. "Your attempt to entrap Mr. Darcy will not work, Miss Eliza. I have been here the entire time."

Bingley, Jane, and Elizabeth jumped at her sudden outcry. "For heaven's sake, Caroline, need you frighten us to death? What, uh, how did you get in here?"

Startled by her brother's voice, Miss Bingley was surprised to discover how many people were within the library.

"And why did you not reveal yourself when I made my entrance to the room, Miss Bingley?" came Mr. Bennet's voice.

"Or when Ja—Miss Bennet and I entered?"

While everyone else was questioning her sudden appearance, Darcy wondered how she had entered the room and what she might have overheard. He moved towards her, his eyes scanning the library for a clue. There, near the corner, a strange shadow on the wall drew Darcy in that direction.

Noticing Darcy's movements, Caroline stepped close to him and placed her hand on his forearm. Darcy jerked his arm away as she began speaking to him, hoping to distract him from his examination. "Why do you not retire, Mr. Darcy? There is no need for you to deal with this so-called *lady*. Charles and I will ensure that our *guests* depart."

Reaching out and pulling the wall farther open, Darcy spoke in a firmly controlled voice. "Miss Bingley, please explain why you forced your way into this room where you were not wanted or needed. How did you know where we were?"

Miss Bingley did not reply.

"Answer the question, Caroline." Her brother's voice was harsher than ever before.

"I was searching for you and Mr. Darcy. When I couldn't find you or either of the elder Misses Bennet, I became concerned. Then I overheard someone speaking of two people in the library. I assumed one of you was being compromised. I chose to come through the servants' passage to protect you."

"Both Miss Bennet and Miss Elizabeth are proper young ladies. Neither would behave in such an inappropriate way." There was anger in her brother's voice due to the insults his sister had hurled at his guests.

Darcy would not be distracted. He needed to know what, if anything, Miss Bingley might have overheard. "How long have you been in the room?"

"For only a second or two before I announced my presence."

"Caroline, you will come with me now, as it will soon be time to say farewell to our guests. We will discuss your behavior in the morning." With poor grace, Miss Bingley followed her brother, with Miss Bennet on his arm, back to the ballroom. Once there, Jane moved to join her mother while the Bingley siblings stood together, waiting for the final dance to conclude before they moved into the entrance hall to say goodnight to their guests.

As soon as Miss Bingley departed, Elizabeth looked at Darcy and her father with a worried expression. "Do you think she discovered what happened? Do I need to worry about her damaging my reputation?"

"I do not believe there is cause to worry," said Darcy with a reassuring smile. "In any case, I shall recommend that Bingley withhold her pin money if she does not discontinue her insults about the Ben–ah–the quality of the neighbors. Miss Elizabeth, are you sure you do not wish to have Mr. Jones examine you? You were barely able to move your arm when I came upon you, and you had tears in your eyes."

"Please do not worry, Mr. Darcy," said Elizabeth.

Her father spoke at the same time. "If you would not mind finding Mr. Jones, sir, I will wait with Elizabeth."

"Of course, sir." Darcy rushed away, eager to be of service to the young woman he found so intriguing.

"Now, Lizzy," said her father as the door closed, "are you truly well?" His left brow arched high on his forehead as he stared at his daughter, waiting for an answer.

Elizabeth easily discerned that her father had seen through her attempts to calm Mr. Darcy with reassurances of her well-being. "My arm is quite painful," admitted his daughter softly.

"And. . ."

Elizabeth's face flushed a deep red. "I am horrified that I was not able to accurately discern the character of the two gentlemen. My assumptions of both were completely incorrect."

"Which of these two things bothers you more?" asked her father with a chuckle.

"Oh, Papa! My hurt ego caused me to say dreadful things about Mr. Darcy, things he did not deserve in the slightest."

"I am sure the gentleman will accept your apology," said her father with another chuckle.

"He has already accepted my apology, but how can I correct the neighbors' opinions when it is my fault they think poorly of him?"

"You are not entirely to blame for his reputation in Meryton, dear. By his own admission, Mr. Darcy is aware that he did not make a good first, or second, impression." Mr. Bennet laughed again. Seeing his sensible, level-headed Lizzy behaving as foolishly as her youngest sister over a gentleman amused her father. However, it also elicited some disturbing reminders that he would lose her one day.

Before Mr. Bennet could amuse himself further at his daughter's expense, Mr. Darcy returned with Mr. Jones.

"How is it, Miss Elizabeth, that you can manage to injure yourself at a ball?" asked the apothecary with a laugh. "I am used to your antics when you are out walking, but what about a ballroom caused you trouble?"

Darcy could see Elizabeth's embarrassment at the gentleman's words and rushed to her defense. "I am afraid it is not a laughing matter, sir. Miss Elizabeth was accosted by someone when she stepped onto the terrace for a brief breath of fresh air." Both Mr. Bennet and Mr. Jones eyed him speculatively, though Mr. Jones' attitude changed as he listened to Darcy's explanation.

"I am sorry for that. Perhaps you would prefer for me to examine you without the presence of the gentlemen."

"That is not necessary," replied Elizabeth, her blush growing deeper. "It is only my arm that is injured. I refused the man's invitation to dance on the dark balcony, but he was unwilling to accept my reply." Elizabeth continued to explain what had happened to her arm.

Mr. Jones checked the pulse in her wrist, which was much faster than usual. Then he gently manipulated her shoulder. He could not feel anything broken or out of place. He asked Lizzy to move her arms in a multitude of ways and was concerned at the limited motion. "I believe you are suffering from a mild strain, so I recommend that you wear a sling for a few days. Hill is familiar with how to fashion one, is she not?"

"Yes," answered Elizabeth, her eyes downcast.

"I will ask the housekeeper to locate something for me to use for a sling now," said the apothecary.

"I am sure it is not necessary," said Elizabeth with alarm. "I cannot be seen leaving the ball in a sling. It will raise too many questions."

"Do not worry, Miss Elizabeth," said Darcy reassuringly. "I will have your cloak brought to you here so that no one will see your arm when you depart."

At his words, Mr. Jones rang for the housekeeper. "If I know my wife, we will be the last to leave, so no one will observe you but our hosts."

"But what will Miss Bingley and Mrs. Hurst say of me if they see me in such a way?"

"Please do not worry about Bingley's sisters, Miss Elizabeth. I will suggest to both Bingley and Hurst that he try your father's suggestion of withholding their pin money. I am quite sure the threat of losing their funds will keep both sisters from speaking."

At that moment, Mrs. Dawson arrived. Mr. Jones explained his need.

"I have just what you require and will return momentarily." The group waited in silence until the servant returned holding a large triangle of what looked to be an old bedsheet. "Will this do, Mr. Jones?"

"Perfect." Mrs. Dawson handed him the cloth and departed. He positioned the material and tied it behind Elizabeth's neck. Moving towards the door, Mr. Jones said, "I will look in on you in a day or so, to check your improvement, Miss Elizabeth."

"Thank you, Mr. Jones."

"Thank you, Jones," echoed Mr. Bennet.

After the gentleman left, Elizabeth looked at her father. "How are we to explain this to Mother? I shall never hear the end of her complaints about my lack of refined manners. However, she and my younger sisters cannot be trusted with the truth if I am to retain any semblance of my reputation."

Mr. Bennet thought for a moment. Chuckling in the hopes of raising his daughter's spirits, he joked, "I have already contained your mother with my threat. I am sure it will work on your sisters as well." Elizabeth laughed with him and noticed Mr. Darcy's attempt to not smile too broadly. Sobering, her father said, "Unfortunately, I shall need to explain the situation to them since they must avoid future contact with Mr. Wickham."

Elizabeth looked doubtful, so Darcy flashed his dimpled smile in encouragement. "Mr. Bennet, would you mind if I remained to keep Miss Elizabeth company while you gather your family to depart?"

"I shall remain a bit longer myself, but perhaps you could retrieve Elizabeth's cloak, or ask Jane to do so."

"Certainly, sir." Darcy stood and bowed to Elizabeth before departing on his errand.

"Lizzy, do you wish me to leave Mr. Darcy with you when I go to gather the family?"

"I believe you should go now, Papa. The behavior of both Lydia and Kitty indicates they imbibed too much this evening. They were making cakes of themselves earlier. I dread to think what they might have done in the last half hour or so in your absence from the ballroom."

"I will do so if it eases your mind. However, be sure to leave the door open when Mr. Darcy returns. We do not wish to compromise either of you."

"Mr. Darcy is a perfect gentleman, Papa, and he would never do such a thing."

Mr. Bennet smiled as he kissed the top of his daughter's head before exiting the library.

Darcy returned shortly. He lay Elizabeth's cloak over the back of a chair before offering to refresh her tea.

"You need not wait on me, Mr. Darcy, but please let me thank you again for saving me. After what you told me of Mr. Wickham, I was quite afraid when I listened to his threats." Elizabeth paused as if deep in thought. "There was one thing that did not make any sense. Mr. Wickham said that his attention to me would cause you pain. I cannot imagine how he could come to such a conclusion."

Now it was Darcy's turn to blush. Having known him from such a young age, Wickham could often read Darcy's feelings with accuracy. Darcy was quiet for so long that Elizabeth did not think he would explain Wickham's words to her. Finally, Darcy looked directly into Elizabeth's eyes. "I would imagine that something in my look at you when we met in Meryton and before I noticed Wickham's presence gave him a clue as to my interest in you." Elizabeth's eyes widened at his words. "I am sure he told you his tale of woe in an attempt to turn you against me. He has always taken great pains to destroy my happiness and hurt those closest to me. I am sorry that my affections caused you to be mistreated so."

MR. COLLINS PLOTS

UNBEKNOWNST TO EITHER, MR. COLLINS WAS listening at the door. He knew that bursting in would only aggravate Mr. Darcy further, so he made a hasty decision. Mr. Collins would put the first part in place that night before retiring and act upon the second part first thing in the morning. He remained listening but would interrupt only if it became absolutely necessary. When he heard the Bennets entering the main hall, he moved away from the door and stood to wait at the base of the staircase, though not quickly enough to avoid Mr. Bennet's observation of his eavesdropping.

Mr. Bennet moved towards his cousin and asked him to escort the ladies to the carriage while he retrieved Elizabeth. When the gentleman was at the door with Mrs. Bennet on her arm, he stepped into the library. In quiet voices, Mr. Darcy and his favorite daughter were discussing Byron's latest work as they waited.

"I do hope your conversation never touched on information of a personal nature, as I discovered Mr. Collins listening at the door."

"Do you think he heard anything of Mr. Wickham's actions?"

Darcy spoke decisively. "I do not know, but you need not worry, Miss Elizabeth. I shall speak to Collins personally when I call to check on your progress tomorrow afternoon."

"Why do you not come earlier? I would like to hear the full story of your relationship with Wickham. It may be necessary to warn the neighbors if he is a danger to the young women in the area. You would be welcome to stay for dinner and visit with Elizabeth afterward."

"Thank you, Mr. Bennet. Would Bingley be welcome should he decide to accompany me?"

"Of course."

Darcy assisted Elizabeth to stand and ensured that her cape covered her sling. He would have liked to have offered his arm and escorted her to the carriage but decided against it. Instead, he bowed over her hand and thanked her for the dances. "I look forward to seeing you tomorrow." Then he accompanied the two Bennets to the door. Bingley was the only one waiting for them. He thanked them for attending his ball and, again, apologized for Elizabeth's injury.

Darcy and Bingley watched as Mr. Bennet looked into the carriage. Coldly, Mr. Bennet said, "Mr. Collins, you will again need to ride on the back of the carriage. It is far too crowded inside." Indistinguishable muttering reached Bingley's and Darcy's ears as an annoyed Mr. Collins exited the carriage and climbed on the back beside the footman. Once the parson was out of the way, Mr. Bennet leaned in and spoke to one of his daughters before assisting Elizabeth into the carriage. The driver flapped the reins on the horses' backs. The gentlemen remained on the porch waving until the carriage turned out of the drive.

The short carriage ride was filled with the loud talk of Mrs. Bennet and her two youngest daughters. Upon arriving at Longbourn, Mr. Collins jumped off the back of the carriage, then rushed into the house and up to his bedchamber. Tossing his coat on the bed, he sat at the writing desk and pulled out a sheet of paper. Dipping his pen in ink, he wrote.

Longbourn
Hertfordshire
26 November 1811

Dear Lady Catherine,

> *It has come to my attention that one of my young cousins is attempting to use her arts and allurements to gain the attention of your nephew, Mr. Fitzwilliam Darcy. She is the lady I first thought to ask to be my wife, but Mr. Darcy said that she would not be a good choice in your eyes. He directed me to the next younger sister.*
> *However, I would never allow your esteemed nephew to be trapped when he is betrothed to your daughter. I will propose to her in the morning and thereby thwart any designs she might have on Mr. Darcy.*
> *I will write again when I have successfully engaged her and will remind your nephew of your desire for his attendance at Rosings Park at his earliest convenience.*

Your obedient servant.
W. Collins

Meanwhile, at Netherfield, Darcy and Bingley sat in the latter's study, each with a brandy in hand, discussing the ball.

"So Darcy, how did Miss Elizabeth get hurt?"

"An uninvited guest attempted to compromise her, but I arrived before anything serious occurred." Everything in Darcy's manner and bearing told his friend he did not wish to elaborate.

"What am I going to do with my sister? Her behavior this evening bordered on incivility."

"Bordered?" Darcy asked with a raised brow. Bingley flushed. "I pray Miss Bingley did not overhear any discussion of the assault on Miss Elizabeth, as she would not hesitate to smear the lady's reputation. Perhaps a threat to her allowance and ability to shop might be a deterrent to her poor behavior. You might suggest the same to Hurst, as his wife is not much kinder to your neighbors."

"That is an excellent idea and one not tried before."

"It was the threat Mr. Bennet used to keep his wife from gossiping. I thought it rather inspired." The two men chuckled before Darcy continued. "Whether she heard anything or not, you may need to speak with her again. Twice tonight she attempted to trap me into dancing with her. Fortunately, I had partners for both sets, which only increased her ire and desperation. You do remember my stance on your sister, do you not?"

"Of course. You will not marry her under any circumstances, and no matter what she tries I will not force you to do so."

"If you did, it might be the end of our friendship. You are aware I tolerate your unmarried sister only because of my affection for you."

"I know, Darcy. I am looking forward to her coming of age, as I plan to set her up in her own establishment. I do not wish her to live in my home once I marry."

"Are you planning to marry soon?" asked Darcy with a quirked eyebrow.

Bingley hesitated to answer, but then screwed up his courage, stating, "My family will not approve, but I love Miss Jane Bennet and I plan to ask her to marry me sometime soon."

"Then you have my congratulations and best wishes. I believe you two are admirably suited. However, when you have learned what you need about running an estate, you may wish to consider a different location for your permanent home. A little distance from Longbourn might allow you and your new bride to settle more comfortably into your marriage."

"That is excellent advice. Now, about your relationship with Miss Elizabeth. It did not escape my notice that you danced two sets with her tonight–the first and supper sets, no less."

"I admire her very much and believe that I will ask her for a courtship. We chanced to meet on Oakham Mount yesterday morning and were able to clear up some of our previous misunderstandings. I was very encouraged that we might move past them when she agreed to dance the opening set with me."

"You know she had no choice if she wanted to dance with anyone."

"I am aware of the rules of society, Bingley, but so too am I able to tell the difference between being accepted for duty versus pleasure."

"Then I wish you good luck." Bingley raised his glass and said, "To the lovely Misses Jane and

Elizabeth Bennet. How fortunate we were to find them in such a small country village."

Darcy raised his glass in the toast. Then, downing the last of his brandy, he said, "Excuse me, Bingley, but I believe I will retire. I am meeting with Mr. Bennet tomorrow morning and am invited to remain for dinner and to check on Miss Elizabeth."

"What time do you plan to leave?

"I plan to arrive at half past eleven. That is late enough for any who might sleep in after the ball."

"May I join you?" asked his companion hopefully.

"Mr. Bennet did extend the invitation to dine to you as well." Darcy chuckled at his friend's pleased look.

Darcy mounted the stairs, ruminating on the events of the evening. He had greatly enjoyed his dances with Miss Elizabeth, but thinking of Wickham's attempts to harm her made his blood boil. Perhaps a letter to Richard was in order.

Arriving in his room, Darcy found his valet, Wilkins, waiting for him. "Wilkins, I believe there is an issue we must address."

"Indeed, Mr. Darcy. What might that be?"

"This evening, Miss Bingley forced her way into the library through the servants' entrance. I was meeting with someone in the library. Do you know where the servants' entrances are to my suite?"

"I do, Mr. Darcy. I have been using the one that allows me access to your dressing room. It is also why I am sleeping there. I place the cot across the opening at night."

"Are there also entrances into my bedchamber?"

"Yes. Two, sir. Do you wish to assist me in blocking them or should I request a footman to help?"

"I will assist, as I do not wish the household to discover our deception. Otherwise, Miss Bingley may find a way around it." Together, they slid the chest of drawers over one of the openings. For the other, they positioned the desk in the way. Then, Darcy placed all of his books on the surface to add weight to the piece. The task completed, his valet assisted him into his nightclothes. Darcy then sat at the desk in his room and began his letter.

Netherfield Park
Hertfordshire
27 November 1811

Dear Richard,

> *I need your assistance. Bingley hosted a ball last evening. Wickham, who has joined the militia here in the village of Meryton, was supposed to be on guard duty during the event. However, he snuck away from his post. When I came upon him, he was forcing himself on a young lady in whom I am interested.*
>
> *If you can join me here, I am hoping that you can use your influence to ensure that Wickham receives the most severe punishment possible. Would you also pick up the packet of his debts from my solicitor? If the military releases him, I plan to have him taken to debtor's prison.*

In good conscience, I cannot allow him to continue to ruin lives everywhere he goes. I am aware that he might mention Georgiana, but I believe that when he is found derelict of duty, and when his debts are discovered, no one here will believe him. I doubt word would travel from this small village to town, so I expect there will be no consequences for my dear sister.

Please send word if you can join me. If not, please arrange the secure delivery of Wickham's debts.

Sincerely,
Darcy

After blowing out the candle on the desk, Darcy climbed into bed. Staring at the ceiling, he wondered how soon Richard would be able to arrive. However, knowing he could do nothing but wait, he turned his thoughts to the beautiful young woman and their evening together. Now that they had worked through their misconceptions, he found conversations between the two of them to be much more natural. They discussed their favorite books and authors, music and their favorite composers, the theater, politics, and the war. Darcy drifted off to sleep remembering the feel of the lovely Elizabeth in his arms after he had rescued her from Wickham. He hoped the day would come when he could hold her like that and never have to let go. He drifted off to sleep with a smile on his face.

A LESSON FOR THE YOUNG LADIES

DARCY WOKE AT HIS USUAL EARLY hour and, after dressing quickly, went for an early morning gallop. He road in the direction of Oakham Mount, though he did not expect to see Elizabeth after such a late night. Man and beast, as one, roamed the picturesque autumn countryside. After a couple of hours of communing with nature, Darcy made his way into Meryton. Stopping at the express office, he surrendered his letter for delivery, instructing the rider to wait for a reply. As Darcy mounted for the return to Netherfield, he noted a man dressed in black with a large white collar entering the village from the other end. There was a feeling of familiarity, but he could not immediately place it. With a shake of his head, Darcy turned and cantered towards Bingley's home.

Returning to Netherfield, he took a long, hot bath. Then, after requesting a tray in his room, Darcy repaired to Bingley's study to attend to some business. As the time to depart neared, Darcy asked that his carriage be made ready. When he passed through the hall, Bingley hailed him from the dining room. "Are you on your way to Longbourn?"

"Yes. It would not do to be late meeting Mr. Bennet if I wish to gain his approval for a courtship with his daughter."

Bingley smiled. "Good luck! Unfortunately, I must have a discussion with my sister before I join you."

"Luck to you as well, Bingley, and stand firm. Remember, you are the head of your family!" With that, Darcy stepped into his waiting carriage for the short drive to Longbourn.

At Longbourn, footsteps on the stair brought Mr. Bennet to the door of his study, where he witnessed Mr. Collins exiting the house with a letter in hand. Thankful that the gentleman had absented himself without needing to be asked, Mr. Bennet asked Mrs. Hill to wake his wife and daughters. He requested their presence in the parlor within thirty minutes or they would lose the next quarter's allowance.

Everyone complied with his threat, though there was considerable grumbling from Mrs. Bennet and her two youngest daughters. Everyone was surprised to find Elizabeth's arm in a sling. Mrs. Hill followed them in with a tray of tea and buns. Once everyone received breakfast, Mr. Bennet stood from his chair and faced his family. "I must make you aware of something that occurred last night. The reason you must know this is because none of you are allowed any further contact with Lieutenant Wickham."

Lydia interrupted, crying, "But, Papa, I am in love with Mr. Wickham and he with me."

"You are too young to comprehend what love is and certainly too young to marry. If you cannot follow my directives, you will return to the schoolroom and Kitty with you."

"I did not complain," whined Kitty.

"Enough! There is not much time to explain what I must. I was fortunate that Mr. Collins had business away from Longbourn this morning, for he must never learn of what I am about to tell you."

"Please explain, Papa," said Jane, ever the peacemaker.

"Last night, your sister stepped onto the balcony for a breath of fresh air. Mr. Wickham, who was supposed to be on guard duty, surprised her and requested a dance. Your sister refused, as propriety demanded, but the gentleman would not accept her words. The lieutenant twisted Elizabeth's arm behind her, causing injury, and attempted to force himself on her." The Bennet sisters gasped in shock and Jane's face paled as she reached to hold her sister's uninjured hand. Elizabeth's face blushed in embarrassment. "Fortunately, Mr. Darcy arrived, saw what was happening, and rescued your sister, while turning Wickham over to his commanding officer."

"Mr. Darcy most likely caused the trouble. I told you how he refused Mr. Wickham a living left to him by Mr. Darcy's father."

"Be quiet, Lydia. I asked Mr. Darcy for his version of events in that very situation. He did not hesitate to explain things and to offer documents signed by Wickham as proof."

"I do not believe you," shouted an angry Lydia.

"Then you will be returning to the nursery. You obviously do not possess the maturity to tell a cad from a gentleman, nor the wisdom to listen to your elders."

"I bet Lizzy caused this on purpose. She liked Wickham, too. She must have been jealous of his attention to me."

"Are you saying you believe your sister is faking her injury or that she hurt herself as part of this scheme you imagine?" Lydia did not reply but glared at her father and Elizabeth.

Mrs. Bennet, who, to this point, sat silently listening, spoke. "That is enough, Lydia. Be quiet and obey your father." Everyone gaped at Mrs. Bennet, who never spoke harshly to her favorite. "Lizzy is often impertinent and aggravating, but she is not a liar. Apologize to your sister."

Lydia looked mutinous, but eventually, her features softened and she said, "I am sorry, Lizzy. I know you would not tell a lie."

Lizzy nodded in acknowledgment.

"I am sorry for my accusations last evening as well, Elizabeth. I am also very sorry that you had to experience something like that."

"Thank you, Mama."

"Wickham's behavior towards your sister is not his only sin. Mr. Darcy indicated that he has been purchasing Wickham's debts for several years. He is also known to be a gambler and womanizer." Gasps came from all of the ladies except Elizabeth, who already knew of Wickham's habits.

Finally, Mr. Bennet's words had an effect on his younger daughters. "To repeat, no one is to go anywhere alone until the militia removes from Meryton. If you arrive somewhere and Mr. Wickham—should he be released from jail—is present, you must leave. If you are ever observed speaking to members of the militia alone, you will not be able to leave the house for anything other than church until I decide otherwise. Once you are allowed from the house, you will not go anywhere without a parent." Here, the eyes of Lydia and Kitty grew wide. "I know that some of you think marriage to a man in a red coat would be wonderful. However, the reality of the situation is that unless they rank above a colonel or receive support from their family, none of them are in the position to take a wife. Most military wives, if they do not follow the drum, live in small quarters without servants and must, therefore, do the cooking and cleaning themselves. There is no money for ribbons and new dresses. Sometimes there is not enough money for food and lodging. I hope that all of you will think carefully about what I am telling you and adjust your behavior if need be. Are there any questions?"

"Why would Mr. Wickham try to hurt someone he calls a friend?" asked Kitty.

"I do not know his particular reasoning. However, there are always men who act like gentlemen in public, but it is just that—an act. You must watch what people do and listen to what they say. Often, their actions will not match their words. In this manner, you discern a person's true character. Now, do you understand my expectations regarding your behavior around Wickham and the other soldiers?" Everyone nodded in agreement. "Lastly, no word of Mr. Wickham's behavior towards Lizzy is ever to be mentioned. If word of this got out, Elizabeth would be ruined and the rest of you by association. Please do not share this information with anyone, be they friend or family. Give me your word that you will never mention this again." Mr. Bennet gave his wife a significant look as he spoke.

"Yes, Papa," came from all of the Bennet sisters.

"Of course, Mr. Bennet," agreed his wife.

"Well, then, you may all return to whatever activities you had planned for the day. I shall be in my study should anyone need me."

Sometime later, Elizabeth sat in the window seat in the small parlor at the back of the house, quietly reading. She enjoyed the peace of the moment. Kitty and Lydia had gone to visit Maria Lucas, while Jane had accompanied their mother to visit their aunt. She was to tell Mrs. Philips the story agreed upon to explain Lizzy and Darcy's presence in the library. They decided to say that a drunken officer had staggered into Elizabeth, forcefully knocking her arm into the stone wall of the house. Darcy, having observed the incident, took Elizabeth to safety and retrieved help.

SURPRISING PROPOSALS

WHEN ELIZABETH HEARD THE FRONT DOOR open, she did not stir, as she knew that Darcy planned to visit her father that morning. Her arm was in its sling, so the book rested on her lap. Absorbed in the story, Elizabeth failed to heed the approach of Mr. Collins until she heard the loud click of the door when it closed.

Holding her injured arm steady, Elizabeth quickly stood. "Mr. Collins, please open the door; it is not appropriate for us to be closed into a room together."

"I need only a moment of your time, dear cousin."

"Open the door first, sir, or you will cause me to call for help." With an oleaginous smile, Mr. Collins turned to the door, opening it a mere inch before facing his cousin again. He saw a fierce scowl on Elizabeth's face.

"Cousin, I came here upon the suggestion of my benevolent patroness to choose a wife from among the cousins who would be homeless upon my inheriting your home. Since arriving, my attention to you has been marked, Cousin Elizabeth, which cannot have escaped your understanding."

"I saw no such thing. However, I did notice the attention you paid to my sister, Mary, last evening. You danced two key sets with her and spent much of your time standing with her when not dancing. I believe she, my mother, and most of the neighbors expect you to make her an offer."

"I doubt anyone noted my brief attention to Miss Mary last evening, especially as I danced with each of my cousins, as well as Miss Lucas. I have had eyes only for you since learning that Miss Bennet is expecting a proposal soon."

"It seems you considered several of us in the short time of your visit, sir." Elizabeth's tone rang with disdain and disgust. "Are we interchangeable to you? In any case, you cannot have developed affection for any of us in such a short time, especially having vacillated over who is your favorite."

"Be that as it may, you are attempting to prevent Mr. Darcy from his duty to his family."

"That is ridiculous, Mr. Collins! My acquaintance with Mr. Darcy is only a few weeks longer than my acquaintance with you. I will not marry anyone unless I feel a deep love and respect for said gentleman, and both of those feelings require time to develop."

"The situation becomes my concern when your actions will cause displeasure to my esteemed patroness and harm to her daughter. Your wishes are irrelevant. Your mother agreed to our marriage, so you will accept me."

"My mother would agree to you marrying any of my sisters, as that will allow her to remain in her home until the end of her life. However, my father is the only one who can grant permission for any of us to marry. I suggest you return your attention to Mary, as she is the sister most suited to you. She is pretty and pious, kind, hard-working, and dedicated to helping the less fortunate—in fact, the perfect parson's wife. Mary might also be willing to accept you, which I will most definitely not. We are in no way suited to one another, Mr. Collins. Now, if you will excuse me, my arm is causing me pain and I wish to rest for a time."

Elizabeth stood to exit, but the gentleman did not move away from the door. "Your father may not wish to grant his consent, but after we are found here alone, he will not have a choice in the matter."

"How can you, a man of the cloth, make such threats? Now, will you move out of my way or do I need to call for assistance?"

When Mr. Collins turned toward the door, Elizabeth breathed a sigh of relief; however, upon hearing the loud click of the lock, she rushed to place the most massive chair in the room between herself and the miscreant standing before her. As he advanced on Elizabeth, she screamed as loud as she could for help. Collins continued to move slowly towards her, and Elizabeth again yelled for help. "Mr. Collins, no matter what you do, I will never agree to marry you. I would rather remain a spinster or go into service than be stuck in a miserable marriage with the likes of you for the rest of my life."

"I doubt your parents would allow that, as it would ruin the rest of your sisters. Consequently, I will look forward to teaching you your wifely duties and how to be an obedient wife. I will break you of your wild ways and independence." Elizabeth's face showed her disgust for the scoundrel in parson's clothes advancing on her.

Elizabeth tried once again to divert him from his intentions. "If you force yourself upon me, I shall report you to the church. You risk losing your living and your future if you continue as you are. Even you cannot be so lacking in sense as to think that you can do this with impunity." She rested her good arm on the chair, keeping it between the two of them. Now he stood just before the chair. Elizabeth cried out, "Mr. Collins, stop this now! I beg you to reconsider!"

A loud creak, followed by a bang, answered her words. Mr. Darcy kicked the door in and grabbed the parson by the shoulder. He spun Collins around and shoved him against the wall beside the damaged doorway, where Mr. Bennet stood. "What do you think you are doing, Mr. Collins?" Darcy ground out between clenched teeth.

"You are interrupting my proposal to my cousin, sir. I would ask you to leave us." Darcy's forearm was against the man's throat, so his words sounded breathy. His face grew even redder.

"Do you wish me to leave, Miss Elizabeth?"

"Most definitely not, Mr. Darcy. I previously turned down Mr. Collins' proposal, but he was unwilling to take no for an answer. He planned to compromise me and force a marriage so that you would be free to marry your cousin."

"We spent some time locked in this room together. Cousin Elizabeth is now compromised."

"Then I will happily rescue her reputation," said Darcy firmly.

"But you cannot do that; you are already betrothed to Miss de Bourgh."

"I will say this for the last time. I am not engaged to my cousin. It is only the desire of my aunt. My mother specifically told me that there was no arrangement with my aunt and that I should follow my heart to find the woman I love and wish to spend my life with."

"But your aunt is your nearest relation. Surely, the desires of such an eminent peeress should supersede your own!"

"My aunt is not my closest relation; my sister is. I am not a de Bourgh or a Fitzwilliam. I am head of the Darcy family. My wishes and desires determine the future of my family—not the delusions of my disagreeable, demanding aunt."

"How dare you speak of Lady Catherine in such a manner. I will ensure she learns of your disrespect, as she should be arriving here soon."

"Why do you think that my aunt will arrive?"

"I sent her an express this morning, warning her of my cousin's attempts to distract you from your betrothal. I promised her that I would remove the distraction by whatever means necessary."

"Should your patroness arrive, you will not be here to greet her. For your attempts to harm my Elizabeth, you will be leaving here today. You are not welcome to return until after my demise. Now, pack your bags and get out. Mr. Hill," called Mr. Bennet. "Please escort Mr. Collins to his room. See that he packs his belongings and leaves the house without delay. If he tries to stall, throw his belongings into the yard."

"You cannot force me from my future home."

"Indeed, I can. It is currently my home, and I am master here."

"Please follow me, Mr. Collins," said Hill as he turned to leave the room.

Darcy looked at the parson, not releasing his hold on the man. "You will not say a word of this to anyone, nor will you make any derogatory comments about Miss Elizabeth, or you shall meet me on the field of honor."

"I am a clergyman, sir. I cannot be involved in such dealings."

"Yet you can threaten and attempt to compromise an innocent young woman. Then I will denounce you for the cad and coward you are. You will be called to account for your actions. Remember my words, Collins. You do not wish to incur my wrath."

Since he was nearly out of breath, the parson could only nod—and barely that, with Darcy's arm pressed tightly against his throat. When Darcy finally released the parson, Mr. Bennet followed his cousin and Mr. Hill out of the room. Darcy pushed the door partly closed and rushed to Elizabeth. Taking her uninjured hand in his, he could feel her body trembling. He assisted her to the settee and took a seat beside her.

"Miss Elizabeth, you are shaking. Are you well?"

"I will be, Mr. Darcy."

"Can I get you anything for your relief? Perhaps a glass of wine?"

"No, I just need a moment."

"What about a cup of tea?"

"That would be wonderful." Elizabeth took a deep breath and sank back into the settee. "I do not know if I was more angry or afraid," she said quietly.

"What did he say?"

Elizabeth related the entire conversation. His thinned lips and hard glare alerted her to Darcy's anger over the situation.

"I am sorry that you were so inappropriately importuned twice in as many days and both times because of me."

"You are not to blame for the actions of others, Mr. Darcy. Please let go of your frustration in this matter." Elizabeth squeezed the hand that was still holding hers.

"For you, Miss Elizabeth, I shall try. Now, I invited my cousin, Colonel Richard Fitzwilliam, to come and help with the Wickham situation. I believe I can help with the Collins situation as well."

"How will you do that, if I may ask?"

"You gave me the idea. You see, my godfather is the Bishop of London. I will send an express informing him of Mr. Collins' behavior. I will not have him stripped of his position, for that might make him desperate. However, I can suggest that he be transferred to a much less desirable location that will keep him too busy to bother your family."

"I would be happy to never speak to or see Mr. Collins again in this life," said Elizabeth earnestly.

"I had hoped to ask you an important question, but perhaps it is not the time."

"I would be happy to listen to anything you wish to say, Mr. Darcy, particularly if it will distract me from my encounter with the dreadful Mr. Collins."

"Miss Elizabeth, would you accept a request of courtship from me? You are the most lovely, intelligent, and interesting young woman I have ever met. I believe we share a great many common interests, and I expect that my opinion that you are the perfect woman for me will be confirmed."

After the experiences of the last two days, this was indeed not what she had expected. However, since their conversation on Oakham Mount the previous morning, Elizabeth was pleased to discover another side of Mr. Darcy as well as the many similarities in their tastes. He was very handsome, responsible, and caring–just the type of man she had always wanted to marry. "I would like that very much, Mr. Darcy, and am delighted to accept your offer of courtship."

Darcy smiled and raised her hand to his lips. He placed a delicate kiss on the back of it. "Would you prefer to remain here while I speak to your father?"

"No, I no longer find this room conducive to relaxing. I shall retire to my room to rest for a bit, but please do not leave without speaking to me."

"Your father kindly invited Bingley and me to dine today. Rest as much as you need. I will be here when you awaken."

As they stepped into the hallway, Mr. Collins came down the stairs, dragging his trunk–thump, thump, thump. Mr. Bennet stood in the opening of the parlor, watching his cousin closely. As Mr. Collins reached the door, Mr. Hill opened it and stepped aside.

Collins looked out the door, then back at his cousin. "Where is the carriage?"

"After your behavior, you are fortunate I did not call the constable on you. You will need to make your way into the village on your own."

Collins sneered at those standing in the hallway. "I should have listened to my father and not attempted to reconcile with your branch of the family. You best pray that your daughters are all married so that your wife will have a home when I take over Longbourn. After the treatment I received during my stay, I will toss them out on the day you die."

"Only if you recall what I said," Mr. Darcy reminded him. "Otherwise, Mr. Bennet will more than likely outlive you." The cold expression in his eye and the quiet tone of the gentleman's voice caused the parson a moment of concern.

"I will inform my patroness of the disgraceful treatment I received here. She will not tolerate such disrespect for those in her employ." Collins turned around and marched through the door, dragging his trunk behind him.

The carriage pulled into the driveway as Mr. Collins was leaving. The ladies acknowledged him as they passed only to receive a harsh glare in return.

When she stepped down from the carriage, Mrs. Bennet wailed, "Where is he going? Did he propose to Mary?" All the while, she fluttered her handkerchief.

"Please come inside, my dear, and I will explain. Jane, you might escort Elizabeth to her room. I believe she would like to rest."

"Mr. Bennet, might I avail myself of your library to write a letter to my godfather, the bishop, while you are speaking to Mrs. Bennet?"

Mr. Bennet's eyes twinkled as he replied, "Of course, Mr. Darcy."

Mr. Hill closed the door as his master escorted his mistress into the parlor. The young ladies retired to their rooms and Darcy settled himself at the desk in the study.

EXPECTED YET UNPLEASANT VISITORS

THE NEXT SEVERAL DAYS PASSED PLEASANTLY, with constant interaction between the parties at Netherfield and Longbourn. Mr. Bennet was happy to agree to Mr. Darcy's request for a courtship. How could he do any less, considering the gentleman had protected his dearest daughter not once, but twice? Mr. Bingley, upon his arrival on the day when Mr. Collins departed, also made a similar request of the Bennet patriarch. Consequently, Mr. Darcy and Mr. Bingley were daily visitors to Longbourn.

On a lovely, unseasonably warm autumn morning, Mr. Bennet sat enjoying a new book in his study. The sound of a carriage on the drive interrupted his peace and quiet. However, the moment he detected Mr. Collins' haughty yet groveling voice, Mr. Bennet put the book down and moved to stand next to Mr. Hill in the entryway.

"What do you think you are doing, Mr. Collins? You were told not to return until after my death."

"I warned you that my patroness would not tolerate the rude behavior I received from you. She is here to instruct you on the proper treatment of a guest and to speak to Miss Elizabeth."

"Be that as it may, you are not welcome and you will not enter my home." The implacable tone would have surprised his family, as they rarely heard it without its usual trace of humor and sarcasm.

"You will allow us both entry immediately," declared the imperious voice of Lady Catherine.

"Whoever you may be, you have no authority here." Mr. Bennet turned away and instructed Mr. Hill to close the door. Before he could do so, Lady Catherine brought her walking stick down hard on Mr. Bennet's shoulder. He staggered under the impact and dropped to his knees. Mr. Hill rushed to assist his master as Mr. Collins and Lady Catherine forced their way into the house.

Mr. Hill called to his wife, who came running. She exchanged a glance with her husband before kneeling next to the master.

"Sir, are you all right?"

He grimaced. "I believe I will need some ice for my shoulder."

Turning to his butler, Mr. Bennet whispered to Hill, "Get help and evict Collins. I don't care how you do it, though tossing him from the house is my preference. I want him out! Also, fetch the magistrate. I plan to press charges for the assault."

As the servants attended their master, Lady Catherine and Mr. Collins went from room to room on the first floor, searching for Elizabeth. When their search of the downstairs rooms proved fruitless, Lady Catherine looked at Mrs. Hill, demanding, "You, there, I want to speak with Miss Elizabeth Bennet. Bring her to me now!"

Darcy, Bingley, and the five Bennet sisters returned to Longbourn to utter chaos. With a sense of worry, Darcy recognized the coach that sat before the entry. A gig also sat in the drive. A dusty, rumpled Mr. Collins beat on the door, and the sound of shouting voices reached them above all the other noise. Darcy moved the parson out of the way as Bingley ushered the girls into the manor. Darcy was the last into the house. He shut the door in Mr. Collins' face before turning the lock. Mary guided her younger sisters up the stairs as the others stood in the doorway to the parlor, trying to understand what was occurring.

Mr. Bennet sat in his favorite chair. He held something to his shoulder as the apothecary checked his pulse and the mobility of his arm. Their only footmen, Tom and Sam from the stables, each had a hand on the shoulder of an unknown older woman who loudly voiced her complaints and demands that she be released.

"What are you doing here, Aunt Catherine?"

"Darcy, I demand that you make these people release me and that you accompany me back to Rosings right now. I will arrange for Mr. Collins to marry you and Anne as soon as we return."

"Aunt, how many times must I tell you that I am not going to marry Anne? Neither of us desires to wed the other. Anne has long been in love with the younger Mr. Woodbury, your neighbor at Kingswood Manor."

"Anne will not waste herself on a younger son. Your mother and I planned for her to be the next mistress of Pemberley. You were formed for each other."

"I know that is not true. Now be quiet, aunt."

"How dare you speak to me in such a manner, nephew." The look Darcy turned on Lady Catherine silenced her, at least for the moment.

Elizabeth moved to stand beside her father. "Papa, what happened to you that you had to call Mr. Jones?" Darcy turned from his aunt to learn the answer to Elizabeth's question.

"I was enjoying a book in my study when the unwelcome voice of Mr. Collins demanding entrance reached my ears. I came out to remind him that he is not welcome here. He and Lady Catherine both demanded entrance, but I refused. When I turned and instructed Hill to close the door, I was struck on the shoulder from behind with a walking stick. I have called the magistrate and intend to press charges."

"How dare you attempt to press charges against me? It is you who should be arrested for trying to prevent me from my purpose. Nephew, I demand that you protect me from this ridiculous man and his charges."

"And just what was your purpose in coming to Longbourn, aunt?" Darcy's tone of voice gave her pause.

"Why, to stop you from making a mistake that you will regret and to prevent you from disgracing the family and failing in your duty to Anne."

"There is no duty to my cousin other than as a cousin. As I am the head of the Darcy family, I am the only one who will decide whom I will marry. Your opinion on the matter is of no importance.

It was at this point that Hill entered the room to announce, "Sir William Lucas and Mr. Smith."

Mr. Collins followed the men into the room and rushed to stand by Lady Catherine.

"Bennet, my old friend, I received your message. As Mr. Smith is also here, I assume it is a legal matter."

"First, I would like that man arrested." Mr. Bennet pointed at Mr. Collins. "He forced his way into my home after being banned and already forcefully evicted once today."

"Is this true, sir?" Sir William stood to his full height, his voice authoritative.

"I came at the request of my patroness, Lady Catherine de Bourgh. She requires my assistance. I am also the legal heir to this home. It is my right to enter it any time I wish." His tone was conceited and haughty.

"You may be the legal heir, but you are not the current master. He is within his rights to ban you from his home if he wishes. Mr. Smith, please take that man into custody."

"You will do no such thing," stated Lady Catherine. "Mr. Collins is my parson. I require his assistance with his cousin. Then he must return to his responsibilities in the parish."

"Your position as a peer of the realm cannot prevent his arrest," said Mr. Smith as he moved to clap the irons on Mr. Collins' hands.

"My lady, please, you must help me," whined Collins as the rough metal closed around his beefy wrists.

"Her being a peeress and you a parson does not make either of you above the law."

"Fitzwilliam, I demand you do something."

"I am sorry, aunt, but there is nothing I can do. You heard Mr. Smith. Your position does not make you above the law."

"Bennet, is this the only issue you needed me to address?" Everyone turned to look at the master of Longbourn and noticed Mr. Jones putting a sling on his arm to keep the weight off his shoulder.

"That depends. I am loathe to insult the gentleman who is courting my Elizabeth. If he can get his aunt to recognize the error of her ways and apologize before departing, there is nothing more to discuss." Everyone turned to look at Mr. Darcy.

"Your choice is before you, aunt. Do you recognize the error of your ways? Will you apologize and return to Rosings Park or do you wish to be arrested and stand trial?"

"I am Lady Catherine de Bourgh. I can do as I wish and you should not interfere." Her authority was somewhat diminished by the fact that the footmen prevented her from standing, though her voice was imperious and her face livid. Mr. Bennet looked at Elizabeth and rolled his eyes at the lady's ridiculous behavior. Lizzy was hard pressed not to laugh but managed to control her reaction out of respect for Mr. Darcy.

"You should do what you must, Mr. Bennet, with a clear conscious," said Darcy. He rolled his eyes at Mr. Bennet and Elizabeth, who looked down to retain her composure.

"Sir William, I attempted to settle this without resorting to the law. However, since no apology is forthcoming, I will not allow this issue to pass. I informed the lady and my cousin that they were not welcome here. However, when I turned my back on them for Hill to close the door, they assaulted me before barging into my home."

Sir William looked at the lady and then at the constable, considering for a moment. "Mr. Smith, is there a place aside from the jail that can hold Lady de Bourgh? I do not feel the jail appropriate for a lady of her age." Lady Catherine visibly bristled at the mention of her age—and not her status—as a reason to keep her from jail. Again, Mr. Bennet and Elizabeth were forced to hide their laughter. As Mr. Smith pondered the situation, Darcy looked at Bingley, a question in his eyes. Bingley wasn't sure what he wanted but nodded, for he trusted Darcy.

"Sir William, Mr. Smith. If it would be acceptable, I believe Mr. Bingley could house my aunt in a guest room or servant's quarters. We will confine her to the room until you can make other arrangements. I shall also contact my uncle, Lord Matlock, and inform him of the situation. As he is the head of her family, she is subject to his edicts."

Sir William and Mr. Smith looked at each other and then at Mr. Bennet. "Is this acceptable to you, Bennet?" asked Sir William.

"I am certain that Mr. Darcy will do as he said, so his suggestion is acceptable."

"If you are concerned, Mr. Smith, you may send a man to watch her room," offered Darcy.

"Thank you, sir. I will allow you to transport her and I will send someone to watch the room so she cannot escape."

"I cannot believe you would allow your illustrious aunt to be mistreated so badly." Mr. Collins' face expressed outrage, though he maintained a hint of subservience.

"Please remove this man from my house, Mr. Smith. I do not wish to listen to his complaints any further."

Mr. Smith grabbed the chains on Mr. Collins' hands and pulled him from the house, then pushed him into the back of the jail wagon.

Sir William looked at Mr. Darcy and Mr. Bingley. "I trust you gentleman to see Lady de Bourgh to Netherfield and contain her as you promised."

"Of course, Sir William." Turning to Mr. Bennet, Darcy said, "I apologize, Mr. Bennet, for the harm that my aunt caused you."

"No apology is needed, sir. You have been nothing but caring to my family."

"Miss Elizabeth, I am sorry this situation prevents us from remaining for supper this evening. I hope we will be welcome to return tomorrow?"

"Of course, Mr. Darcy. Thank you for a delightful morning. We look forward to seeing both you and Mr. Bingley again tomorrow."

Darcy took his aunt by the elbow. "Come along, aunt. I believe you should offer your apologies for your behavior today."

"I will do no such thing. I am the injured party here. I will ensure that my brother makes Mr. Bennet suffer for his actions against me."

"That is enough, aunt. If you cannot behave as a lady of your station should, then you deserve whatever punishment you receive. When you are in jail for your deeds, I will assist Anne in marrying Mr. Woodbury and taking her place as the rightful mistress of Rosings Park. I believe Uncle Lewis left the estate to her in his will. Anne kindly allowed you to retain your position longer than she should. Obviously, running your own estate gave you the impression that your word is law even outside of your small part of the country."

"Rosings is mine, not Anne's. . ." began Lady Catherine.

"That is enough, aunt. You will be silent until you are in your room."

Darcy tugged her arm and took her out to her carriage. After helping her in, he closed her inside before giving instructions to her staff. "Hawkins, please retrieve my and Mr. Bingley's horses from the stables and tie them to the back of the carriage. Smith, you will be taking us to Netherfield Park, where my aunt will await the arrival of my uncle. Turn right out of the drive, pass through the village, and then turn right at the road on the far side of the village."

"Yes, Mr. Darcy."

Darcy remained standing outside the carriage, waiting as Bingley farewelled Jane. When his friend arrived, Darcy said, "Thank you for allowing this, Bingley. I am sure she will be contentious and cause more disruption than I would wish."

The two gentlemen entered the carriage. Darcy knocked on the roof just before the vehicle began to move.

"That was quick thinking on your part, Darcy. I shall go straight to London and swear out a charge against Mr. Bennet."

"You shall be going nowhere, aunt, except to your so-called cell. I was serious when I said you would be contained at Mr. Bingley's estate until this situation is resolved. You will be locked in a bedchamber and the only services you will receive are the delivery of your meals. You will attend to yourself, as no maid will be provided. The staff will be informed that you are not permitted from your room, nor are any of them to assist you. A footman will accompany the maid when your meals are delivered, to ensure you do not escape. I will be sending an express to Uncle Henry tonight. You should consider yourself lucky that you will be in a comfortable bedchamber rather than a cell. Bingley, please instruct your staff about these requirements. You shall also need to ensure that Miss Bingley does not assist my aunt. Threaten her with charges should my aunt escape."

"Certainly, Darcy."

"When your uncle arrives, he will have something to say about your dreadful treatment of me, nephew."

"I would be more concerned with his words to you, aunt, when he discovers you assaulted a gentleman enough to cause injury and forced your way into his home."

Lady Catherine looked concerned for a moment before her bravado returned. "That man is of no consequence and had no right to deny me, a peeress."

"With that mindset, you are saying that if some disgruntled duke showed up at your door and forced his way in while striking you in the process, you would allow his actions to stand?"

His aunt sat up straighter and said, in her most imperious tone, "No one has the right to enter Rosings Park without my permission."

"That is true of any home. You are no different from a housebreaker forcing yourself into Mr. Bennet's home and assaulting him. If he had not already done so, I would call for the magistrate and constable."

"You would not dare!"

"Indeed, I would. If you cannot control yourself and behave appropriately, it will be necessary to force you to do so."

"How can you speak to me, your nearest relation, in such a manner?"

"As I have informed you many times, aunt, you are not my nearest relation. Georgiana is. I would also not place our relationship above that which I share with the Fitzwilliam family. Lastly, you have no say in the decisions I make for the Darcy family." By this time, the carriage arrived in front of Netherfield. "Bingley, why do you not go in and arrange for a room for my aunt? I will wait here with her until the room is ready and then escort her up. Please ask Mrs. Dawson to give me all the keys to my aunt's room. I will accompany the servants who deliver her meals."

Bingley jumped out and rushed up the stairs. Dawson opened the door to admit him before he reached the entrance.

"Where is Mrs. Dawson? I need to see her forthwith."

"Of course, sir." The butler looked to a footman, who headed to the door leading to the kitchen.

"You wished to see me, Mr. Bingley."

"Yes, Mrs. Dawson. I need the guestroom farthest from all the other occupied rooms prepared as promptly as you can. Please do not repeat this to anyone else, but it is being used to hold someone who cannot go to the jail because of age. The only service she is to receive is the delivery of meals. All the keys to the room shall go to Mr. Darcy. He will accompany the maid and footman who deliver the meal. Please provide water with which to wash each day, but no baths or maid service. Please notify me when the room is ready."

"Yes, sir." Mrs. Dawson scurried away, asking for three additional maids to join her in the yellow room.

Darcy sat in the carriage, facing his aunt. He saw no point in conversation, as she would not, or could not, see the error of her ways. As he waited to accompany her to her room, he thought of what he would write in the letter to his uncle.

After about twenty minutes, Bingley appeared at the window of the vehicle. "The room is ready. I ensured that no one is about between here and Lady Catherine's chamber. Mrs. Dawson will meet us there to give you the keys and take any additional orders you wish to give. I instructed that she gets her meals delivered and clean water every day with which to wash. I did not think you would wish her to have a bath. What about keeping up the fire? Should we leave a bucket of coal, or do you wish to allow someone to enter to build it up regularly?"

"Thank you, Bingley. I will decide when I see her reaction to her room." Darcy stepped down and turned to assist his aunt. She refused his assistance, but he caught her when she stumbled. When Lady Catherine's feet were firmly on the ground, she yanked her arm away and marched into the house. Lady Catherine looked about for a servant to take her things, but no one was in sight.

"Your attempt to join the landed gentry will fail, as you seem to have no concept of welcoming a guest to your home." The lady's tone was cold and disapproving.

"Instead of complaining, you should be thanking Mr. Bingley. He arranged it so that no one would see your shame as you go to your room."

The lady sniffed. Darcy took her elbow and moved Lady Catherine towards the stairs. They followed Mr. Bingley up two flights and to the far end of the guest wing hall. The housekeeper stood there waiting. She opened the door to the room as the others reached the chamber. Bingley entered, followed by Lady Catherine and Darcy. Mrs. Dawson entered and closed the door behind her.

Lady Catherine looked about. "This room is too small. I will require a larger suite, one with a sitting room attached."

"You are not a guest, aunt. Be glad you are in a comfortable room, not a cell.

"Water and towels are on the stand, your ladyship."

"I require a bath."

Darcy glared at Lady Catherine. "You would not be permitted a bath in jail, aunt, so you will not receive one here. You will have a bucket of coal so that you can maintain your fire. Your meals will arrive at. . ." Darcy looked at Mrs. Dawson for an answer.

"Breakfast by half-past nine, dinner by half-past one, and supper at seven. When would you like the trays picked up, my lady?"

"I will ring when I am through."

"Mrs. Dawson, you may pick up the tray half an hour after delivery. I am sure my aunt will not need longer."

"Yes, Mr. Darcy."

"I require a maid to assist me," demanded Lady Catherine.

"No, aunt. You are not here to visit. For all intents and purposes, this is your jail cell."

"Here is my key to the room, Mr. Darcy. Miss Bingley retains the other set," Mrs. Dawson said. "You or Mr. Bingley will need to ask her for the key, as I did not know what reason to give her as to why I needed it." Darcy looked at Bingley, who nodded.

"That is fine, Mrs. Dawson. I thank you for getting the room ready so quickly. I hope that it did not cause you and your staff any inconvenience. I should also apologize in advance, for I am sure that my aunt will not be kind to those who serve her. I will provide a bonus for all those whom she abuses."

"I thank you very much, sir."

Darcy nodded to Bingley and the housekeeper, who both departed. "I am sorry it has come to this, Aunt Catherine. I will see you later." The lady did not deign to reply, so Darcy walked out and locked the door behind him. Darcy leaned on the wall across from the room and waited. When his aunt said nothing, he breathed a sigh of relief. As he turned to walk away, the man sent by the constable approached.

"I am Jacob Smith, sir. My father asked that I guard the prisoner being housed here."

Darcy extended his hand to the young man. After explaining what services would be allowed, he handed the key to the young man. "Mr. Bingley will bring you the other key to the room." Then, with a weary look, he turned and walked away.

Darcy entered his chamber and rang for Wilkins. After refreshing himself and changing for tea, Darcy sat at the writing desk and pulled out his supplies. Half an hour later, he summoned the butler to his suite.

"Please ask my groom, Woods, to meet me in Mr. Bingley's study as soon as possible. I will also need the services of one of Mr. Bingley's footmen to take a letter to the express office." Darcy descended to the study and paced as he waited. The footman arrived first, so Darcy handed him a letter addressed to Anne de Bourgh. "Please take this to the express office for delivery. Ask the rider to wait for a reply." Darcy resumed his pacing while waiting for his groom. When Woods entered, slightly out of breath, Darcy handed him the letter. "I need you to deliver this to London directly. Please wait for a reply and return as soon as possible. If Lord Matlock is not at home, please ask his staff where to find him, as it is urgent that he receive this."

"Yes, Mr. Darcy. Is there a particular horse you wish me to take?"

"Take Maximus. He is the fastest one in the stables. I will use another of Mr. Bingley's horses until you return.

With a nod, the groom tucked the letter into an interior pocket and hurried from the room.

MISS BINGLEY DEPARTS

As HE ENTERED THE DRAWING ROOM, Miss Bingley rushed forward and grabbed his arm. "Mr. Darcy, we are so pleased you are with us this afternoon. You spend far too much time at Longbourn, as does Charles," she said with a glare at her brother.

Darcy looked at Bingley and raised a brow. The look his friend returned was one of disappointment, but he nodded his head, a frown on his usually smiling lips. "I am sorry you find my behavior disappointing, but I suggest you accustom yourself to it, for it will not be changing anytime soon. I enjoy the company of Mr. Bennet, with whom I share excellent conversation and challenging games of chess."

"Is Mr. Bennet the only draw for you or are you attracted to a pair of fine eyes as well?" Miss Bingley's smile was stiff and her eyes suspicious.

"Yes, I am, and I am currently courting Miss Elizabeth Bennet. As such, I would prefer that you cease hanging on my arm whenever I enter a room. I would also appreciate it if you ceased making derogatory remarks about the Bennets. If you do not wish to know your neighbors better, perhaps you should return to town. You might find a suitable match during the little season. I am sure Bingley and I will survive quite well here on our own."

Caroline was astounded by Mr. Darcy's words. A courtship. He was telling her to find another candidate for a husband. Was it possible that he was serious? She had devoted four years to garnering his attention, and it had all been a waste of time.

"You cannot be serious! Why would you lower yourself to become entangled with a young woman so far beneath you and one whose family is a disgrace?"

"Miss Elizabeth is a gentleman's daughter, and I am a gentleman. That makes us equals in my mind."

"But she has no style or accomplishments. She is not trained to care for a home along the lines of Pemberley. She will disgrace and embarrass you! You cannot be serious in your intentions."

"I am well aware of your opinions, Miss Bingley, and as I said, I prefer that you keep them to yourself. Though I do not need to explain myself, let me make my feelings very clear. Miss Elizabeth is kind, intelligent, and well-read. She is also well-spoken and stands up for what she believes. She helps her father handle their estate and tends to the needs of the tenants. I believe Miss Elizabeth possesses all the qualities I desire in the next mistress of Pemberley."

"Charles, are you going to let Mr. Darcy throw his life away on such an undignified country family?"

"I do not know what you expect me to say to him, Caroline. Darcy is a grown man and capable of making his own decisions, just as I am. In fact, Darcy is not the only one currently courting a Bennet. I began courting Miss Jane Bennet on the day after the ball. That is when Darcy's courtship also began."

"Charles, both Louisa and I told you that Jane cares nothing for you. She is pursuing you at her mother's command. You could do so much better, brother. I insist you return to town. We will both look for suitable mates before the end of the little season."

"Were you not listening, Caroline? I am courting Miss Bennet and am not interested in returning to London. Though Darcy is right that you should do so. If the Hursts wish to assist you, I will write to Aunt Agnes, asking her to visit and serve as my hostess. I would not wish to lose the opportunity to entertain the Misses Bennet due to the lack of a hostess."

"That is an excellent idea, Bingley," agreed Hurst. "Why do you ladies not see to your packing this afternoon? We can return to town in the morning. There is still almost a month of the little season remaining. If you put your mind to it, you might find yourself engaged by Christmas."

"Come, Caroline, let us go begin our packing," said Louisa, rising.

Caroline stared at everyone in the room as if they had all lost their minds. *Can this be happening? Am I willing to give up on Darcy so easily? If I remain, could I prevent the gentlemen from making such life-changing mistakes? Will Mr. Darcy change his mind if he is exposed to me further?* Looking at his implacable expression, Caroline got her answer.

"Of course, Louisa. I am sure that a stack of invitations is waiting for us at Hurst House. Perhaps there will be an event we can attend tomorrow evening." Caroline gathered her dignity around her as she stood. With her head high, and her nose even higher, she followed her sister from the room.

When she left, Hurst got up and poured three glasses of brandy. Handing one to each of the gentlemen, he said, "Congratulations to you both. You have found lovely women during this sojourn in the country. May the courtships progress as you wish, bringing you both a lifetime of happiness. I could not be more pleased that you both stood up to Caroline. It has been a long time coming. I will do all I can to ensure she finds a good mate as soon as possible. Getting her out of my house will be good for my marriage, as well." The gentlemen raised their glasses in salute, and each settled to ponder his private hopes.

Miss Bingley remained in her room the rest of the afternoon, supervising the maid as she packed. At dinner, she was unusually quiet. It was one of the most pleasant meals Darcy could recall in the present company. Caroline's anger at Darcy and her brother was palpable, but she contained it and refused to speak to anyone.

As the gentlemen sat over their after-dinner port that evening, Darcy said, "Bingley, I should have mentioned this sooner. I hope you will not mind, but after the ball, I contacted Richard to come and help me with the Wickham situation. Then, earlier today, I invited my uncle to Netherfield to help in dealing with my aunt. Would it be too much trouble to have your housekeeper prepare three rooms? I do not imagine my aunt will wish to remain behind if there is a chance to put Aunt Catherine in her place."

Darcy's smile made Bingley chuckle. He had met Lady Matlock, who, though charming, could be quite intimidating when the situation required. She was the sort of no-nonsense woman who would not appreciate the ridiculous posturing of her sister-in-law. "That is no problem, Darcy. I will alert Mrs. Dawson before retiring. Perhaps while Lady Matlock is here, she would consider hosting a dinner to which we could invite the two eldest Misses Bennet."

"If the situation with my aunt does not take long, and they do not have any pressing engagements that require a quick return to town, I am sure she would be willing to preside as the hostess for one dinner. I would like them to meet Miss Elizabeth."

When the gentlemen returned to the drawing room after dining, Miss Bingley moved to the pianoforte. That night, she played tempestuous pieces that Darcy assumed matched her disappointment and mood rather than the love songs she usually forced Darcy to endure. It was a pleasant change from her uncomfortably forward behavior.

When the group retired for the evening, Darcy made his way to the guest room where his aunt resided. "How are things going, Jacob?"

"Quiet, sir, which is not what I expected after my father's report. She did harangue the maid about the meal she received, but other than that, the lady has been quiet.

"If she asks, you may tell her I checked in on her. However, I do not wish to speak to her, as that might incite her anger. Is there anything you need to help you get through the night?"

"Mr. Bingley's housekeeper promised to provide plenty of coffee throughout the night.

Moreover, should I doze, I am a light sleeper, so she will not get past me."

Darcy gave directions to his room. "Should my aunt cause problems during the night, do not hesitate to send for me. Good night, Jacob."

"Good night, Mr. Darcy."

As Darcy enjoyed dinner at Netherfield, the Matlock's butler interrupted their quiet evening at home to deliver an urgent message.

"An express arrived for you, my lord."

"Thank you, Dunston."

Lord Matlock looked at the seal before breaking it. He scanned the contents once, then read it again more slowly.

"Blast. What was Catherine thinking to behave in such a manner? I am afraid, my dear, I must depart for Hertfordshire at first light."

"What has your sister done now, Henry?"

Instead of answering, Lord Matlock handed the letter to his wife to read.

"I really must wonder if Catherine is in her right mind, husband. Such behavior would suggest she is not. It was good of Darcy to keep her out of jail, but she must be held accountable for her actions or they will only get more out of control. Let us finish our meal. Then I will arrange for our packing, while you arrange for the carriage. We can be in. . ." Lady Matlock referred to the letter. "Meryton by mid-day."

"Did I hear you say you are going to Meryton?" questioned Richard, their younger son, as he entered the dining room. "I was stopping in to tell you that I planned to go there tomorrow.

Did Darcy ask for your help with Wickham as well?"

"Wickham? What has Darcy to do with that scoundrel?" asked Lord Matlock.

"No, we are going to help him with Catherine," answered his mother at the same time.

"What is Aunt Catherine doing in Meryton?"

"Stop," said Lord Matlock. "We are talking at cross-purposes. Have you eaten, Richard?"

"Not yet, Father."

Lord Matlock asked the footman to lay a place for Richard. Once he was seated and served, the earl dismissed the servants. When the room was empty, he looked at his son. "What has Wickham done now to cause Darcy to request your help?"

Richard explained what had occurred and the information about Wickham's arrest. "I was away on assignment when the letter arrived. Today, I arranged for leave and spoke with Darcy's attorney, picking up the paperwork he asked me to bring. With any luck, the militia will punish Wickham for dereliction of duty. He could be hanged or transferred to the front. If they do not, Darcy is determined to have him sent to debtor's prison. With the amount of debt Wickham has accumulated over the years, he will be old and gray when he gets out. If we are lucky, he will not survive that long." There was menace in Richard's tone. "So, what is it that Aunt Catherine has done for Darcy to require your assistance?"

Lord Matlock handed the letter to his son. Richard read through it, his face showing his disgust. "Father, it appears that Aunt Catherine has lost her mind."

"That is exactly what your mother said." Richard smiled at his mother, who did not mince words, particularly when it involved his Aunt Catherine.

"Richard, do you know what Darcy could mean by the postscript?"

The colonel looked at the note at the bottom of the letter. "I am not sure, Mother, but it is about time he took that wretched woman in hand. Can this be handled before we leave? I do not think Darcy would ask it of you were it not important."

"A quick note or two and I am sure word will have spread throughout the ton before our return. Now, let me think. Which ladies would be best suited to sharing this information?" The satisfied grin on his mother's face caused laughter from both Richard and his father.

Turning to the earl, Richard said, "What are we going to do with Aunt Catherine?"

"We will discuss it on our drive there in the morning. Richard, why not ride with us? We can tie your horse to the back of the carriage."

"That sounds excellent, Father. It will be much more comfortable in the carriage than on horseback in this cold weather."

They finished their meal and separated to attend to their various duties in preparation for their trip on the morrow.

While the three Matlocks began their journey to Meryton, Anne de Bourgh received an express. Recognizing the seal as that of her cousin, Darcy, Anne was extremely curious as to the contents. Darcy rarely wrote to her because of her mother's wishes for them to marry. They both feared that Lady Catherine would regard any correspondence as a sign of their agreement with her plan. Upon opening the letter, Anne read through it quickly, her face growing red the more she read. However, as she reached the final paragraph, a broad smile appeared on her face. Had Darcy been present, Anne would have kissed him for the suggestion! Trusting Darcy and the Matlocks to deal with her mother's ridiculous behavior, Anne sent a note to Lawrence Woodbury, suggesting a meeting at their usual spot. With any luck, she would be a married woman by the end of the day. She and her husband would settle into the master and mistress suites of the estate before her mother even returned. Darcy's letter recommended banishing her mother to the dower house upon her return and restricting her contacts.

A short time later, Anne stood with the man she loved. She explained her cousin's letter and suggestions. Dropping to one knee, he held both of Anne's hands in hers. "My darling, Anne, I never thought this day would arrive. I love you with all my heart. Will you do me the great honor of marrying me?"

"Oh, yes, Lawrence! I cannot wait to be your wife, but whom can we find to marry us?"

"I am sure that Mr. Whiteside, who has the gift in Father's living, will be happy to perform the service. Do you wish to dress? We can speak to him together. Perhaps he can perform the service immediately."

They returned to Rosings and Anne called together the housekeeper and butler. She explained that, per her father's will, she was the current mistress of Rosings and had finally decided to take her rightful place. Both of these servants had been with the de Bourgh family prior to Sir Lewis' wedding to Lady Catherine. She had never been popular with the servants, but they stayed to protect his daughter. Consequently, the Hendersons were delighted with Anne's words. She requested moving her mother's items to the dower house and having her own belongings moved to the mistress's chamber. "As my mother will be away for a few more days, it seems the perfect time to make this transition." The two old retainers could not contain their pleasure at Anne's words.

A few hours later, everything was prepared to welcome the new mistress and her new husband. Life at Rosings would be very different in the future. One of Anne's first tasks as the new mistress was to send an express to Darcy, informing him of the changes at Rosings Park.

Darcy took a tray in his room for breakfast. He did not know what mood Miss Bingley might be in that morning. She had managed to maintain her calm the previous evening, but Caroline Bingley was not known for controlling her temper for extended periods. He did not wish to cause her more discomfort than necessary. Darcy stood in the shadow of his drapes when he heard the carriage pull up to the door at about half-past ten. From where he stood, he could see the Hursts and Miss Bingley. The latter glanced up at his window with a ferocious, vengeful look on her face. The expression made Darcy grateful he had added that last note to his letter to the Fitzwilliams. He did not doubt that Miss Bingley would attempt to ruin Elizabeth's future in the ton. He sincerely hoped that Miss Bingley would be successful this season in finding someone she would like to marry, as it would remove her from his life and that of her brother.

Soon after the carriage departed, Darcy and Bingley rode to Longbourn for a visit. They were quick to request the company of their ladies for a walk. They asked Mary to chaperone. When they reached the gardens, the two couples separated. Bingley and Jane wandered arm and arm through the rose garden while Darcy and Elizabeth headed to a bench in the walled portion of the garden.

As soon as they were seated, Elizabeth asked, "How did things go with your aunt yesterday?"

"She was surprisingly calm. She complained that her room was too small and she had plenty to say about the quality of the meals, but I reminded her that she was under arrest, not on holiday." He went on to explain the other arrangements that had been made for her.

"Based on what I have learned of her from you and Mr. Collins, as well as her outlandish behavior in our parlor yesterday, I cannot imagine her keeping her displeasure with such things to herself. Do you think that, with time, she has accepted that she was at fault?"

"Lady Catherine admitting to an error? I doubt that is what she is doing. I would imagine she is storing up her complaints and will unleash them on my uncle when he arrives. I received a reply to my express to my uncle. They will be arriving before tea this afternoon. Unfortunately, today's visit will, again, have to be short." Darcy was pleased with the look of disappointment that appeared on Elizabeth's face. "Bingley and I plan to ask my aunt to act as hostess for a dinner at Netherfield while she is in residence. I am anxious to introduce you to my Aunt and Uncle Fitzwilliam.

"Why would your aunt need to act as hostess?"

"I was able to convince Miss Bingley to return to London and look for a marriage partner. She was not pleased to learn of our courtship, but I managed to make her understand that her hopes would never be gratified."

"How did she take the loss of all her dreams?"

"Far better than I could have imagined. Miss Bingley was unusually quiet last evening, and I avoided her departure so as not to push her ability to control her temper. Hurst is anxious for her to marry as well so that he gets his home and his wife back. Miss Bingley has added many complications to their life. Bingley told her that if she did not find a husband, he would set her up in an establishment of her own or she could live with their maiden aunt in Manchester. He does not want her to live with him after marrying."

"Do you think, in her disappointment, she will speak poorly of my family and me?"

"I honestly do not know. However, since I asked my aunt to let it be known not to invite her to events based on a relationship to me, anything she says will look like sour grapes and hopefully have little impact. Also, she is aware of her brother's courtship. Therefore, anything she might say would reflect badly on her, as your sister will eventually be part of her family. I am sure Hurst will do everything he can to prevent her from being her own worst enemy, as it would also affect him and Louisa. I hope she does not set her sights too high, as it will end in disappointment and she would still be a burden to her family."

"I am sure her absence will make your stay more comfortable. I know, from my stay at Netherfield, that you never enjoyed her attention. It amazed me that she was oblivious to your true feelings."

"Miss Bingley seems to believe that belittling those around her will increase her appeal to society. However, belittling her betters—members of the society she so wishes to join—makes her a laughingstock among them. If she cannot accept her position as the daughter of a tradesman, she will continue to be a laughingstock and probably a spinster. No one of the first circles will accept her, even with her dowry."

"Not even a cash-poor peer?"

"Well, perhaps, but I truly hope not, for as a peeress, her behavior will get even worse."

"Perhaps we can find a better use for our brief time together today than discussing Miss Bingley."

"I am at your disposal, Miss Elizabeth. Your wish is my command." Darcy extended his arm to her and they began to stroll around the gardens, discussing whatever came to mind.

When it came time to depart, the gentlemen kissed the ladies' hands and rode away. Jane and Elizabeth stood on the porch, waving until the men turned out of the long drive.

DEALING WITH LADY CATHERINE

BINGLEY WATCHED DARCY PACE THE FRONT drawing room while waiting for the arrival of the Matlocks. When he heard the carriage on the drive, he walked out to meet his relations. "Uncle Henry, Aunt Elaine, I am pleased to see you. I hope your trip was comfortable. Richard, I expected you a few days ago, but I am glad you are here. Please join me inside."

"If you were writing to both Richard and your uncle, you have had your hands full of late."

"You have no idea, aunt. As I said, I am glad to see you, but I am sorry it is under such distressing circumstances." Darcy led them into the drawing room. "You all remember my friend, Bingley." After exchanging greetings, everyone sat down. "Bingley was present when everything with Aunt Catherine occurred. He and I had just returned with the Bennet sisters from a trip into the village. You may speak in front of him. Bingley was kind enough to allow Aunt Catherine to be held here rather than at the jail."

"I hope she did not make trouble for your staff."

"Not so far. According to Darcy, Lady Catherine has been unusually quiet since arriving here."

"I cannot believe that Catherine would go so far as to force her way into a stranger's home."

"As I said, Mr. Bennet was willing to let the situation go for an apology and her departure, but

Aunt Catherine's response was, 'I am Lady Catherine de Bourgh. I can do as I wish, and you should not have interfered.'"

"Did Catherine really assault the gentleman?"

"Mr. Bennet's shoulder is injured, and his arm is in a sling. I offered to help him with his estate during his recovery."

"Why was a gentleman of such short acquaintance willing to allow your aunt to go without punishment?" asked Lady Elaine.

Darcy hesitated, though only a moment. "Because I am courting his daughter."

Lord and Lady Matlock were surprised at his reply, but also somewhat relieved. "You are interested in a young lady?"

"I am, aunt. She is the most intelligent, kind, witty, and beautiful young lady of my acquaintance."

"Well, I, for one, would like to meet such a paragon," said Richard. "If she captured your heart, she must be quite something."

"Indeed, she is!"

"Perhaps once things are settled regarding Catherine, you might invite your young lady to tea," suggested his aunt. Uncle Henry had not spoken up to this point, but as he had not erupted in anger either, that was a good sign.

At that moment, the housekeeper arrived with the tea tray.

As they drank their tea, the conversation remained general, with many questions asked of Bingley about estate management. They spoke of his family and the neighbors they had met. Bingley proudly announced his courtship of Jane Bennet, the elder sister of the girl Darcy was courting.

After tea, Bingley busied himself about the estate with the steward as Darcy and the Fitzwilliams discussed what to do with Lady Catherine.

"What do you think set Catherine off on this enterprise?"

"Her miserable excuse for a parson."

"How is her parson involved with this?" questioned Lord Matlock.

Darcy explained to them Mr. Collins' visit and plans, at Lady Catherine's urging. "He set his sights on Miss Elizabeth, but I talked him into a more appropriate choice in her next younger sister. Then, the day after the ball, after observing me dance with her, Mr. Collins decided it was his duty to remove the temptation and possible roadblock to my marriage with Anne. I interrupted him while he attempted to force his kisses on Elizabeth. Mr. Bennet threw him out, demanding he not return until after his death. When I interrupted them, he warned me that Aunt Catherine would be arriving soon, as he had written to her, telling her about the threat to my engagement."

"How many times have we told her, there is no engagement between Darcy and Anne?" asked Lord Matlock.

"Obviously, not enough," answered his wife. "What do you think she is planning that made her so quiet?"

"I fear she is storing up her anger to unleash on you, uncle."

Lord Matlock sighed. "I guess we had better face her and get the matter resolved."

"Wait. What was the reason you needed Richard's assistance?" It was Lady Matlock who spoke.

Darcy's expression grew dark and a scowl appeared on his face. "Bingley hosted a ball a week or so ago. I noticed Elizabeth escape to the terrace after a harangue from Mr. Collins. I followed to check on her, only to discover Wickham attempting to assault her. He has joined the militia stationed here in Meryton and was assigned guard duty for the night so that he could not attend the ball. After knocking him out and helping Elizabeth inside, I turned him over to his colonel. He is in the guardhouse at present. The militia will decide what to do with him. If they release him with no real penalty, I will arrange for his incarceration in Marshalsea. Richard retrieved the packet from my solicitor of the debts I purchased over the years."

"Why do you and Richard not take care of Wickham, and leave your aunt to me? Preventing Wickham from causing more harm will make the world a better place," said Lord Matlock. The four of them looked at each other with nods of agreement.

While Richard had their horses prepared, Darcy led the Matlocks to Lady Catherine's room. He introduced them both to Jacob Smith, who was back on duty, and explained their purpose. "I believe that Mr. Bennet will agree to whatever we can work out to remove my aunt from his family's presence. While they are talking with my aunt, I must attend to another matter."

"Of course, Mr. Darcy. However, my father's approval is necessary for whatever is worked out."

"That is perfectly acceptable." Jacob unlocked the door and the Matlocks entered the room. Before Jacob could relock the door, Lady Catherine's outraged voice sounded through it.

Young Mr. Smith leaned against the wall and folded his arms as he shook his head.

"Brother, I think Fitzwilliam has taken leave of his senses or been bewitched by that Bennet girl, for he allowed me to be arrested and locked up here for over a day now. What took you so long to arrive? I demand you release me!"

"I do not think it is Fitzwilliam whose senses are in question, Catherine. How could you assault a gentleman and force your way into his home?"

"I asked to meet with his daughter and he denied me. I needed to speak to her and inform her that Darcy is already engaged to my daughter. If need be, I will buy her off."

"Catherine, you have been told numerous times that Darcy and Anne are not going to marry. Neither of them wishes it."

"But it was the fondest wish of his mother and me."

"No it was not, Catherine," said Elaine Fitzwilliam. "I was Anne's best friend. Her only wish for her children was that they should find someone who loves and cares for them."

"Best friend, ha! As sisters, we were closer than Anne ever was with you."

Lord and Lady Matlock looked at each other. The latter actually rolled her eyes. "Catherine, George Darcy told me there was no agreement for the marriage. Anne's dying wish was that her children find a love like she and George shared. However, your wishes for Darcy aside, what made you think you had the right to assault Mr. Bennet and force your way into his home?"

"He is a nobody. I am a peeress. How dare he defy me? His estate is worth very little. His daughters offer nothing in the way of dowry or connections. The estate is entailed upon my parson, for heaven's sake. She is not worthy of stepping into our sister's shoes."

"That is for Darcy to decide, not you. When offered a chance to avoid prosecution, why would you not apologize?"

"Why should I, a peeress, apologize to a lowly country squire?"

"You broke into his home like a common thief!"

"How dare you say that, Henry. I did nothing for which I must apologize."

"Do you truly believe that, Catherine?"

"Of course!"

"You are the one out of your senses, Catherine. I will call for our family physician to come and evaluate you. Then we must decide whether you will go to Bethlehem hospital or whether keeping you at home with a nurse and guards is possible."

"How dare you say such a thing to me, Henry? Perhaps it is your sanity that is in question."

"I am not the one who broke into a gentleman's home and assaulted him. If you cannot see the error of your ways, we will leave you here until the doctor arrives." Lord Matlock turned and knocked at the door, asking Jacob to release them. Before the door opened, a vase crashed into the wall by the doorframe. Lord

Matlock successfully put his arm up to protect his face, but a shard of the porcelain lodged in the side of his hand.

"Henry!" cried Elaine. Hearing the crash, Jacob opened the door and rushed into the room. Lady Matlock hurried to her husband's side. She slipped her hand into his pocket and pulled out his handkerchief, which she wrapped around his hand to staunch the flow of blood. She hurried her husband into the hallway, calling for assistance. A footman came running. "Please send someone for the doctor. My husband is injured."

"We have only an apothecary, my lady, but I will send someone immediately." He hurried away.

As Lady Matlock directed her husband towards the stairs, the housekeeper came in her direction. "How can I assist you, my lady?"

"Lord Matlock's hand is injured. We must clean the wound and bandage it. I asked a footman to fetch the apothecary."

Mrs. Dawson asked a passing maid to fetch her medical bag. "Follow me. I will take you to the sitting room between your chambers." The Matlocks followed the housekeeper. Noticing a decanter, Lady Matlock poured her husband a healthy dose of brandy. As she handed the cup to Lord Matlock, the maid arrived with Mrs. Dawson's medical bag. The housekeeper unwrapped the handkerchief from his hand. Looking at the wound, she pulled a cotton bandage from her kit and folded it several times. As she pulled the shard from his hand, Mrs. Dawson pressed the pad firmly against the cut. She moved it briefly and could tell that the wound would require stitches. The best way to clean it would be to wipe it with alcohol. She moved to the brandy decanter and tipped it onto a clean cloth.

"I'm afraid this might sting a bit, your Lordship." He gritted his teeth as the alcohol came in contact with the open wound. "I am afraid there is nothing we can do until the apothecary comes, as the wound requires stitches."

AND NOW FOR WICKHAM

MEANWHILE, AT THE MILITIA ENCAMPMENT, DARCY and Richard sat before Colonel Forster's desk.

"It is a pleasure to meet you, Colonel Fitzwilliam."

"I came at Darcy's request to assist with the Wickham situation. What will his punishment be, Colonel Forster?"

"The most I can do is to flog him for abandoning his post. Because of his short term in the militia, I can release Wickham without any complications."

"However, that does not stop him from preying on other innocent young women. That is what we must stop. Wickham has been leaving debts since his Cambridge days. I purchased all those of which I am aware. Did you check to see if he accumulated debts here in Meryton?"

"I did. Here are the debts I discovered." Colonel Forster handed the list to Darcy.

"I will stop on my way out of town and pay these. Would it be possible for you to allow some of your men to ride to London with Colonel Fitzwilliam to deliver Wickham to Marshalsea?"

"When would you like to travel?"

The colonel looked at Darcy with a raised brow. It was Darcy who answered the question. "I believe it will be two or three days before the other business to which we must attend is concluded. That will give you the time you need to carry out the military justice and allow us to complete another issue with which we are dealing."

"Please send a note the day before you wish to leave. If you ride into the camp, I will arrange for a four-man guard ready to accompany you."

"Thank you, Colonel." Richard extended his hand to Colonel Forster.

"I will arrange for his flogging tomorrow. That way, he will be able to ride by the time you wish to depart."

When Darcy and Richard returned to Netherfield, Darcy observed Mr. Jones descending the stairs. He acknowledged the gentleman as he rushed past him and into the house. As soon as he entered the door that Dawson still held open, Darcy demanded, "Where are my aunt and uncle?"

"I believe they are in the sitting room attached to their suite, sir."

Darcy rushed up the stairs, Richard following, though he did not understand his cousin's urgency. Darcy knocked on the door, barely waiting for a response before entering. "I saw the apothecary leaving. What happened?" Noticing the bandage on his uncle's hand, he queried, "How did your injury occur?"

"It is just a small cut. When we went to talk to Catherine, the first words out of her mouth were that you were out of your senses or bewitched for having treated her that way. She demanded to be released. I asked her why she had done what she did and why she would not apologize. She gave me essentially the same answer she gave you. I am beginning to think that Elaine and Richard were both right. I believe Catherine has taken leave of her senses. I sent a note to Dr. Townshend. Once he examines her, we can decide what to do with her. I would prefer to keep her condition from getting out. If necessary, we will keep her at the dower house with a nurse and guards."

"But how did you get injured?"

"After her ridiculous answer, I told Catherine I would call the doctor to examine her. When I turned to exit, she threw a vase at the door. I put up my hand to protect my face, but a shard buried itself in the side of my hand. It required a few stitches, that is all."

"We should have stayed with you to face Aunt Catherine." Guilt was written on Darcy's face and in his tone. "The Wickham matter could have waited an hour or two."

"Nonsense," said Lady Matlock. "No one would expect that Catherine would behave in such a fashion. Ensuring that Wickham can no longer harm this family, or anyone else, is far more important than dealing with your ridiculous aunt. What was the outcome of your meeting?"

Richard answered his mother's question. "He will be flogged tomorrow for abandoning his post and then returned to the stockade. In two or three days, when everything is resolved with Catherine and we have met Darcy's ladylove, four guards and I will accompany him to Marshalsea."

Lord Matlock addressed his son. "I am glad sufficient guards will accompany you as you transport him. We all know how wily Wickham can be. What is the amount of his debt, Darcy?"

"Including the debt he incurred in Lambton in the month of his service in the militia, it is over six thousand, five hundred pounds. That does not include any debts of honor."

"Good heavens!" cried Lady Matlock. "You purchased all of those debts?"

"I did. Wickham often used the Darcy name when he set up accounts. Therefore, when he would skip out on the debts, they would send bills to me. Had he not disappeared after the Ramsgate incident this past summer, I would have had him arrested then."

"Why did he not run away upon encountering you in Meryton?"

"Because he is unaware that I purchased all his debts."

"Is there a solicitor in the village who can prepare the paperwork necessary for Wickham's admittance to Marshalsea?" wondered Lord Matlock.

"Mr. Philips, who is Miss Elizabeth's uncle, is the local solicitor. I will contact him tomorrow to get the process started."

"Well, as there is nothing more we can do today, I believe we could all use some tea and a change of topic," said Lady Matlock.

They family adjourned to the main drawing room, where Darcy stood and pulled the bell cord to summon a servant. Once tea was delivered and everyone was seated, Darcy made his request. "Aunt Elaine, might you consider acting as Bingley's hostess for a night or two so that we might invite the eldest Misses Bennet to dine with us? I would like you all to meet Miss Elizabeth."

"I would be happy to do so. However, please ask Mr. Bingley to mention the event to his housekeeper before I can make any plans."

"What is it I must discuss with Mrs. Dawson?" Bingley asked as he entered the drawing room.

"My aunt agreed to act as hostess so that we can invite Miss Bennet and Miss Elizabeth to dinner."

"Excellent! My thanks, Lady Matlock." Before seating himself, Bingley pulled the cord to summon a servant. When the housekeeper arrived, Bingley addressed her. "Mrs. Dawson, Lady Matlock has agreed to act as my hostess during her stay. Would you please meet with her to plan a meal to which we would like to invite Miss Bennet and Miss Elizabeth?"

"Of course, Mr. Bingley. When would you like to hold the meal?"

"Would the day after tomorrow be acceptable? Perhaps they could come to tea tomorrow, where the introductions can be made."

Mrs. Dawson and Lady Matlock exchanged a look and a smile. Ah, the eagerness of young love. At a small nod from the countess, Mrs. Dawson said, "I believe we can make that work, sir."

"I will write out the invitations and send them this evening. Perhaps, Mrs. Dawson, we could discuss the menu after supper."

"Yes, my lady. I shall come to you here while the gentlemen are enjoying their port, if that is convenient."

"That would be fine, Mrs. Dawson."

RESOLUTIONS AND INTRODUCTIONS

THE NEXT DAY, AS NOON APPROACHED, the residents of Netherfield relaxed in the drawing room, awaiting the arrival of Dr. Sullivan, who served as the physician for the Darcy and Fitzwilliam families. They heard the sound of hoofbeats on the drive and expected the doctor to appear. Instead, Dawson stopped before Darcy and extended a tray with a letter on it.

"This express just arrived for you, Mr. Darcy. The man was told to wait for a reply."

"Thank you, Dawson."

Darcy quickly recognized the writing and hurried to break the seal.

Rosings Park
Kent
6 December 1811

Dear William,

I am sorry that Mother has imposed herself on you in such a shocking manner. I would not have thought it possible she would ever physically assault someone. I did as you suggested and am now Mrs. Lawrence Woodbury. The servants are already cleaning the dower house, and Mother's maid is packing her belongings for the move.

Does it make me a terrible person if I hope that Mother's situation is not resolved expeditiously? For so long, I lived under her domination; I wish to enjoy the start of my marriage in peace.

Congratulations on your courtship. I hope that you and Miss Elizabeth will find happiness together. Please send word on the outcome of Mother's situation.

Fondly,
Anne Woodbury

As Darcy relayed the information in the letter to the three Fitzwilliams, Dawson announced the doctor.

"Ah, Sullivan. Thank you for coming, man. Please be seated. I will explain the situation before taking you to the patient." As first Darcy and then Lord Matlock told of the events of the last two days, Dr. Sullivan shook his head in bemusement.

"Well, unless a tremendous change occurred overnight, I believe I can give you a diagnosis now. You may accompany me, but please do not speak. I will put similar situations to Lady Catherine. Depending on her answers, I will then ask her about her behavior at Longbourn."

Everyone accompanied Dr. Sullivan, but only Darcy and the earl entered Lady Catherine's chamber. The doctor's questions were much the same as those that Lord Matlock and Darcy had asked on the two days previous.

"I will ask the housekeeper to send you up some tea, my lady. It will help to soothe you during this difficult time." The doctor stepped into the hallway and beckoned the family to follow him.

When they returned to the drawing room and everyone was seated, the doctor spoke.

"It is my professional opinion that Lady Catherine can no longer tell right from wrong and is a danger to herself and others. While you decide her future, we need to arrange for some tea laced with laudanum for her. She will be easier to manage if she is under light sedation going forward. As I see it, you have two options. First, I know of a doctor who runs a very humane facility, though how Lady Catherine might interact with the others could be an issue. Second, I can recommend several nurses you could employ to care for her at home or another private location."

"As Anne married during her mother's absence, I believe having Catherine at the dower house with a nurse or two would be the best option. I assume we will need several strong footmen at the house to assist should my sister become recalcitrant."

"When I return to town, I will send the list of nurses to you by express. You can contact them to set up interviews."

The earl stood and offered his hand to the doctor. "Thank you for making the trip, Sullivan. We will look forward to receiving the information you have for us."

Lady Matlock offered the man a meal that he gratefully accepted before returning to London.

"I must admit to being relieved," said Darcy. "Anne will not be burdened with her mother and can look forward to a happy marriage with her new husband."

Now that the situations with Wickham and Lady Catherine were complete, the afternoon saw the residents of Netherfield awaiting the arrival of Jane and Elizabeth Bennet, who would join them for tea. Speaking quietly amongst themselves, the Fitzwilliams awaited the ladies' arrival in the blue drawing room. "I never thought I would see the day when Darcy was so intrigued by a woman," said Richard with a chuckle as he watched his cousin pacing before the front steps of the manor, awaiting his ladylove.

"Nor I," laughed his father. "How many ladies of the ton have you thrown at him, my dear?"

"Too many to count," replied the countess. "I cannot wait to meet Miss Elizabeth and find out what makes her so superior to the ladies already among his acquaintance."

Upon the Bennet sisters' arrival, and after introductions took place, the conversation was a bit stilted, as Lord and Lady Matlock attempted to take the young lady's measure. However, Elizabeth could not help responding to the colonel's banter and rather far-fetched stories of his exploits in the army. With her wit and humor shining through, Elizabeth responded to his sallies and the entire group relaxed. Though they held up their end of the afternoon's conversation, the earl and countess spent a great deal of time observing their nephew and his interactions with and attention to Miss Elizabeth Bennet. Both were delighted with what they found. Though quite different in temperament, Elizabeth and William had personalities that complemented each other nicely. The young ladies stayed but an hour, so the older couple was anxious for the next day's dinner, where they would have the opportunity to learn more of the young lady who had stolen their nephew's heart.

The next evening, Darcy sent his carriage to retrieve Jane and Elizabeth Bennet for dinner at Netherfield. They gentlemen, again, waited on the front steps for the ladies' arrival. Both looked forward to a delightful evening of polite conversation and pleasant company. There would be no Miss Bingley, with her snide comments about the Bennet ladies. There would be no Mrs. Bennet, with her crass comments and loud voice. Darcy felt confident that his relations would see even more of Elizabeth's value and would happily welcome her to the family once he proposed. He wondered how long it would be before Elizabeth's feelings for him equaled his affection for her.

At that moment, they heard the sound of carriage wheels. Their wait was over. Moments later, Bingley and Jane entered the room, followed by Darcy and Elizabeth. They exchanged pleasant greetings as they sat waiting for the call to dinner. All three Fitzwilliams had immediately liked Elizabeth the previous afternoon. Lady Matlock's affections grew when she recognized a kindred spirit in Elizabeth Bennet. The evening did, indeed, pass pleasantly, with lively conversation on a wide variety of topics. As the gentlemen lingered over their port, Lord Matlock spoke to Darcy.

"I approve of your choice, William. I believe you and Miss Elizabeth will be very happy together."

"I could not agree more, uncle." This time the earl could not contain his laughter at the silly grin worn by his usually somber nephew.

"When will you ask for her hand?"

"I know my feelings, and have for some time. However, our relationship is still new, and I do not wish to rush Miss Elizabeth."

The earl looked at his nephew. "I do not think you will be made to wait long. From my observances, I believe the young lady is quite smitten."

In the drawing room, the ladies discussed the theater and current events. When the gentlemen rejoined the ladies, Lady Matlock took charge. "I hope you will write to me, Miss Elizabeth, of your plans, as we wish to be in attendance at the wedding."

Elizabeth looked down as color suffused her face.

"Aunt!" cried Darcy with a blush. "We only recently began courting."

"Do you not plan for this courtship to end in marriage?" The countess gazed at her nephew with a raised brow.

"Of course, it is my hope," he answered without hesitation.

"And you, Mr. Bingley?"

"It is my hope as well," he answered with his usual enthusiasm. Jane blushed at the gentleman's words, a small smile on her face.

"Then once that takes place, you must let me know when you plan to arrive in London. I wish to give a ball to celebrate your marriages. I will also sponsor both of you so that you may make your curtseys to the queen."

"That is very kind of you, Lady Matlock, but it is not necessary," said Jane with quiet dignity.

"Oh, but it is my pleasure to do it. I wish to be the one to launch the most beautiful and fascinating young ladies to join the ton in some years."

"We appreciate your thoughtfulness, my lady," said Elizabeth, "and would not dream of denying you your pleasure." Lady Matlock eyed the younger lady with a raised brow before she and Elizabeth both burst into giggles. Darcy and the earl looked upon their respective ladies with bright smiles and eyes that appeared somewhat misty.

When the time came, the sisters reluctantly departed. Darcy and Bingley accompanied the ladies home, as it was after dark, but soon returned to Netherfield. They enjoyed a nightcap and a game or two of billiards with the colonel before retiring.

COMINGS AND GOINGS

SO IT WAS THAT FOUR DAYS after their arrival, the elder Fitzwilliams departed, taking with them a very subdued Lady Catherine. Her morning tea, liberally laced with laudanum, made transportation to her new home easier, as well as prevented those in the carriage from having to bear her endless arguments and complaints. The couple would remain at the dower house long enough to interview and select the nurses to attend Lady Catherine. Anne and the Rosings butler hired four large, strong men who would serve as both footmen and guards for the dower house. The house was ready to receive its occupant when they arrived. Lady Catherine was taken to her bedchamber in the dower house, where her maid waited to care for her. The earl and countess interviewed nurses the following day, selecting two to attend the earl's sister. For Lady Catherine's safety, as well as the protection of others, the first-floor exterior doors and windows were kept locked at all times. The two nurses, one for day and one for night, ensured Lady Catherine received constant supervision. So, less than a week after she barged into Longbourn, Lady Catherine took up residence in the dower house with her new caregivers and staff in place.

After settling the former mistress of Rosings into her new home, Lord and Lady Matlock spent a night with their niece to ensure that Anne had all she needed in her new position, as well as to congratulate her on her wedding. The couple was amazed at the changes Anne had accomplished in only one week. The armaments were gone and, much of the ridiculously uncomfortable furniture had been removed. The main drawing room had been repainted to eliminate most of the ornate gold leaf. The room now appeared beautiful and inviting.

"I cannot believe how much you accomplished so quickly, Anne."

"I always hated these overdone rooms. There is much still to do, both for Rosings and the tenant homes, but we can finally restore Papa's home to its original glory."

"I am sure Lewis would be very pleased," said Lord Matlock.

"You must invite us for a visit when it is completed. If you continue as you have begun, it will be a lovely and inviting home."

"Thank you, aunt. Now you must tell me everything about William's young lady." The happy expression and excitement in Anne's voice brought comfort to both of the Matlocks. They worried greatly for Anne's happiness under her mother's iron rule, but in only a week of freedom, she had blossomed into a completely different young woman. Gone was the appearance of ill health, some of which was a ruse to deceive Lady Catherine and allow Anne some peace. In its place was a radiantly happy new bride.

After a delightful meal—another change to Rosings—and several hours of catching up, the Matlocks happily departed knowing that Anne and her new husband would enjoy a bright future.

As the carriage containing the elder Fitzwilliams turned onto the road, Darcy observed a rider in a militia uniform coming up Netherfield's drive. Having farewelled his parents, Colonel Fitzwilliam stood beside his cousin as they waited for the rider to reach them. The young lieutenant dismounted and saluted Richard before advancing to hand the letter to him.

"Thank you," said Richard. The young man saluted again before remounting and turning his horse to return to the encampment.

Richard and William entered the house and made their way to the library before Richard broke the seal on the message.

_____shire Militia Camp
Meryton, Hertfordshire
11 December 2011

Dear Colonel Fitzwilliam,

It is my duty to inform you that Mr. Wickham presented with symptoms of fever and infection this morning. He is in no condition to travel. The doctor expects it will be at least two weeks before he may be fit to do so, if he survives the infection.

His wound did not initially appear unusual, but now several of the stripes are inflamed and pus oozes from them. I have never seen a flogging result in such infection and cannot explain the cause.

I am sorry for any inconvenience this may cause you or Mr. Darcy. Not knowing the length of your leave, I will notify Mr. Darcy if and when Wickham can travel.

Respectfully,
Colonel J. Forster

"Well, this may be a blessing in disguise. The world will be a safer place when rid of Wickham and his disgusting behavior."

"I cannot but feel sadness for the waste of a life that my father believed had promise. However, you are right; it may be the simplest solution to our problem."

"Until such time as he can travel, I am free to remain and enjoy your company, cousin. My leave extends into the new year."

"Would you consider traveling to Pemberley to retrieve Georgiana? That way, I can stay with Elizabeth. After all the difficulties we endured recently, I dread leaving her. We are to spend Christmas here at Netherfield and, of course, I wish Georgie to be here as well. I am sure Bingley would welcome you, should you wish to join us."

"I would be happy to collect Georgiana. It has been too long since we spent any time together. Is Georgiana expecting you? Will she be prepared to travel?"

"Yes, I sent an express a few days ago, telling her when to expect me. She should be prepared to travel the day after you arrive. However, if you would like to take a day or two to recover before the return trip, you are welcome to do so."

"My thanks, cousin. I always enjoy a stay at Pemberley, but I do not doubt that Georgiana will be anxious to return and to meet her *future sister*." They chuckled at this, as her letters to both men were full of questions about Elizabeth and her sisters.

"While you have your man pack, I will write a letter for you to take to Mrs. Reynolds. I wish for her to make some changes to the mistress' chambers before I bring Elizabeth to Pemberley."

The two men parted to their duties. Within an hour, Richard was mounted on his horse and headed north.

Elizabeth sat in the window seat of her room, trying to read. Darcy would depart that day for Pemberley to bring his sister to Hertfordshire. Elizabeth could not understand the feeling of melancholy. Her opinion of William had only recently improved. Why did the thought of his absence cause her such disquiet and unhappiness?

Shortly thereafter, she heard a knock on the front door. A moment later, William's resonant voice requested to see her. Not bothering to wait for the summons, Elizabeth rushed from her room and flew down the stairs to the hall below.

"Mr. Darcy, what are you doing here? I thought you would be on your way to Pemberley by now."

"A message came that changed things, so Richard has gone to get Georgiana in my place. I was loath to leave you after all the turmoil of late."

"Was not Colonel Fitzwilliam to take Mr. Wickham to town today?"

William laughed. "Perhaps we might sit down before I explain things."

"Oh, I am sorry, Mr. Darcy. Come with me." Elizabeth turned and led him down the hall to the small sitting room at the back of the house. Having avoided the place since the incident with Mr. Collins, she paused before entering and took a deep breath. William gave her an encouraging smile and they stepped through the door together, then sat on the settee as close as propriety would allow. Their hands rested between them on the fabric, where no one would see, their fingers almost touching.

William explained the events of the morning, including the letter describing Wickham's condition.

"How are you taking this new information, Mr. Darcy? I am sure that learning of Wickham's condition caused distress of some kind?" asked Elizabeth, her voice quiet and filled with concern for this exemplary gentleman.

"As I explained to Richard, my feelings are mixed." He gave Elizabeth the same accounting he had given the colonel.

"I am so sorry. I cannot imagine how difficult this must be for you. Please know that I am here for you if you need anything." She placed her hand on his, squeezing it. Darcy felt his heart swell at her actions. Perhaps his uncle was correct and it would not be much longer before he could propose.

As it was now December, there were events—teas, dinners, and dances, among others— several times a week, allowing the courting couples to spend many hours together. The gentlemen usually spent the morning at Longbourn and enjoyed the mid-day meal with the family. The couples would often meet again in the evenings at one of the neighborhood gatherings. As was typical of courting couples, they tended to ignore the majority of those around them in favor of time spent together.

The only disturbing event during that time was the arrival of a note from Colonel Forster, announcing that Wickham had succumbed to his injuries. Darcy could not bring himself to allow Wickham to be buried at Pemberley, nor did he think that Lambton would be the right place after the debts and ruination Wickham had left in the village. Therefore, Darcy paid for his body to be transported to Kympton and buried in a corner of the churchyard there. He worried about how to tell Georgiana of the event, but Elizabeth promised to assist him if he so desired.

A week after his departure, Richard Fitzwilliam returned to Netherfield with Georgiana Darcy. Bingley arranged for Jane and Elizabeth to join the party at Netherfield to welcome her and allow the ladies to become acquainted.

While Georgiana refreshed herself after traveling, Darcy gave Richard the letter from Colonel Forster.

"Good riddance," declared Richard. "Of course, it is like the coward to take the easy way out of his punishment."

"Now, Richard, I doubt the experience was pleasant," said Darcy wryly. "After spending a week with her, how do you think Georgie will take the news?"

"I believe she is much improved from the events of this past summer. She may experience sadness, as you did, for the wasted life, but I do not believe it will overly upset her."

"Elizabeth offered to help me break the news if need be. Do you think Georgie would take it better from us or would Elizabeth's presence be helpful?"

"I would allow her to meet Elizabeth today without knowledge of Wickham. We can explain it before she retires tonight." Darcy agreed with his cousin's suggestion and they let the matter drop.

Georgiana was descending the stairs when the Bennet sisters entered Netherfield Park. As Darcy and Bingley waited to greet the ladies, Darcy took Elizabeth's hand and led her to where his sister stood at the bottom of the staircase.

"Georgiana, allow me to present Miss Elizabeth Bennet, the young lady whom I am courting. Miss Elizabeth, this is my sister, Miss Georgiana Darcy."

The young ladies exchanged curtseys. Elizabeth was the first to speak. "I am so pleased to meet you, Miss Darcy. Your brother has told me so much about you. You are quite fortunate to have such a devoted older brother. As for myself, I have only sisters."

"I should like to a have a sister someday," responded Georgiana shyly.

Darcy offered an arm to both ladies and led them into the drawing room, where Richard, Bingley, and Miss Bennet awaited. Bingley introduced Jane. Again, the ladies exchanged greetings.

Bingley asked Jane to pour the tea for everyone as a maid passed among the guests with cakes and sandwiches. Once everyone had their refreshments, the conversation turned to the travels of the newcomers.

With that topic exhausted, Bingley addressed Georgiana. "The aunt whom I invited to serve as my hostess is ill and could not make the trip. I wondered, Miss Darcy, if I might impose upon you to act as my hostess while you are here. My housekeeper is quite competent, and I am sure that Miss Bennet and Miss Elizabeth would be willing to assist you, if necessary."

Georgiana paled at the request. A look of nervousness on her face. Unsure how to answer, she hesitated, giving Darcy a chance to interject his opinion. "I think it would be an excellent opportunity for you to practice, Georgie. Mrs. Annesley can provide you with all the assistance you need. She can make it part of your lessons."

The young lady's companion nodded and smiled encouragingly at her charge. "It would be an excellent opportunity to learn, Miss Darcy. You are surrounded by friends who will not demand too much of you."

"An excellent idea, Mrs. Annesley," seconded Richard with a smile.

In a quiet voice, Georgiana asked, "Do you intend to do much entertaining, Mr. Bingley?"

"Other than opportunities to invite the Misses Bennet to join us, I plan only one dinner."

Georgiana noted the friendly and supportive faces around her. Taking a deep breath, she said, "I would be happy to help you, sir."

The group discussed a variety of topics over the next hour or more. By the time the ladies departed, Jane, Elizabeth, and Georgiana were addressing one another by their Christian names.

Before retiring for the evening, William and Richard informed Georgiana of Wickham's fate. Because of her questions, they were required to explain what had led to the flogging. "I am glad to know that Miss Elizabeth was not harmed. I am also relieved that Mr. Wickham cannot harm my reputation or anyone else's ever again."

The day after Georgiana's arrival, William received a surprise visit from his godfather, a bishop who assisted the Archbishop of Canterbury.

"I was astonished at the contents of your letter, William. We had received complaints from the parishioners at Hunsford. Apparently, Mr. Collins was unable to maintain the secrecy necessary for one in his position and had reported everything he learned to Lady Catherine. Said lady did not hesitate to interfere in the affairs of everyone around her. However, I was greatly distressed to learn that his faults extended to an attempt to compromise a young lady to assist his patroness."

"You are quite familiar with my aunt's over-inflated self-worth." The bishop nodded, and Darcy went on to explain the outcome of Lady Catherine's visit and her current situation.

"Where is Mr. Collins at present? Is he still in the village jail?"

"As far as I am aware, he is, sir."

"Well, then, I believe I shall have to visit Meryton. Would you like to accompany me?"

"Only if you need my presence. I would much prefer to hit the man than converse with him. He is a ridiculous person and I am surprised he managed to graduate from university."

"Is he truly that bad?"

"I shall say no more and let you form your own opinion, sir, but I look forward to hearing that opinion upon your return." Darcy could not help the chuckle that escaped him. "Do you wish to speak to Mr. Bennet before you visit with Mr. Collins? I would be happy to introduce you."

"Shall I also meet the young lady you are courting?"

"I would be happy for you to make her acquaintance." So saying, the gentlemen left in the bishop's carriage for Longbourn with Darcy's horse tied to the back.

After Elizabeth was presented to the bishop, they all joined Mr. Bennet in his study. Darcy's godfather found the young lady delightful and enjoyed her father's dry wit and humor. A brief discussion occurred before the bishop departed. Darcy remained to walk in the garden with Elizabeth for a short time before returning to Netherfield and Georgiana.

An hour and a half later, Darcy's godfather returned to the manor house. He was shaking his head as he entered the library where Darcy sat. "I shall need to investigate who conducted his ordination. Never in my life have I met a man less suited to be a clergyman." The bishop collapsed into a chair as he spoke. Darcy stood and poured a brandy for the man. He handed it to the bishop before returning to his chair.

"I wonder if the same person ordained all of Lady Catherine's parsons, as the three I met were quite similar."

"The imbecile actually tried to convince me that it was his duty to do everything asked of him by his patroness. I informed him that Lady Catherine was found to be incompetent and was now at the dower house under guard. I thought the man would break down in sobs." Darcy merely rolled his eyes and waited for his godfather to continue. "After questioning, I found it clear that he should not be in charge of a parish. I informed him that he was being reassigned as the curate of a church on the edge of the London slums, where even his foolishness cannot cause harm to his parishioners. He begged and pleaded to retain his post, so I informed him that he was lucky to retain a position in the church at all."

"How did he react to that?"

"As you would expect. I did consider releasing Mr. Collins but feared that he would only make himself more of a nuisance to Mr. Bennet and his family. I did not feel that to be fair."

"I appreciate that, sir. I would not wish him to be anywhere near Elizabeth in the future. How will his transfer take place?"

"If you could write to Miss de Bourgh and request that his effects be packed and sent to the address I will provide you, I will take him to his new church upon my departure tomorrow, providing your friend will offer me a room for the night."

"One has already been prepared for you. I will also be happy to write to Anne, who is now Mrs. Woodbury." With the business of Mr. Collins now completed, the gentlemen relaxed into their chairs and caught up on the events of their lives since their last meeting.

"I do hope you will ask Miss Elizabeth if I might take part in your marriage service. I am happy you have found such an excellent young woman with whom to share your life. I know your father and mother would both have liked her very much."

A PAIR OF PROPOSALS

THE WEEK OR SO BETWEEN GEORGIANA'S arrival at Netherfield Park and Christmas passed in a blur. There was an indoor picnic in the Netherfield conservatory and shopping trips to Meryton. These usually included much laughter and giggling as the shoppers tried to secretly select gifts when the recipients were often present.

Mr. Bingley hosted the family from Longbourn for dinner on Christmas Eve. Georgiana did an outstanding job planning the meal and decorating several of the rooms in the house. After a magnificent feast, the sexes separated, as was the custom.

As Mr. Bennet raised his glass to his lips, Darcy spoke. "Mr. Bennet, I wonder if I might request a moment alone with Miss Elizabeth when we are through here."

The older gentleman took a sip of his brandy and savored it for a moment before answering. With his left brow raised, he gazed at Darcy with a speculative gleam. "I assume it is a matter of some importance?"

Darcy did not hesitate to answer. Holding Mr. Bennet's gaze he said, "Yes, sir, it is essential to my happiness." The pink color of his ears was the only indication of the gentleman's emotions.

"Then you have my permission."

"I would like to request a moment with Miss Jane as well." Bingley received the same look before also receiving permission from the Bennet patriarch.

With permission granted, the gentlemen were eager to rejoin the ladies. Mr. Bennet, knowing there would be no lively debate over their after-dinner port, delayed their departure only briefly as he enjoyed a few more leisurely sips of his drink. When he stood to rise, the younger men rushed out of the door before him. They entered the drawing room, walked directly to where Jane and Elizabeth sat, and requested their company for a moment or two. Offering the ladies their arms, the men exited the room with their ladyloves.

In the hallway, they separated. Bingley and Jane took the hall leading to the small conservatory. Darcy asked Dawson for Miss Elizabeth's outerwear. He assisted her with her cloak and held her gloves as she tied her bonnet on her head. New snow dusted the world with white while big flakes lazily floated down from above. With her arm tucked in his, Darcy led Elizabeth to a bench surrounding the frozen fountain. In summer, the heady scent of the many nearby rose bushes would provide a delightful perfume to the air.

Once Elizabeth was seated, Darcy took both of her hands in his and dropped to one knee. "Elizabeth Diana Bennet, from almost the first moment I saw you, you became the focus of my world. Your beautiful eyes mesmerized me and the magic of your laughter claimed my heart. Your beauty defies words and your effervescent mind is a delight to my senses. I look forward to our lively interactions. I love you, Elizabeth. Would you do me the very great honor of accepting my hand in marriage?"

From the moment the handsome gentleman before her knelt, Elizabeth found it difficult to breathe. The loving words he spoke brought tears to her eyes. Those happy tears spilled over onto her cheeks as she breathlessly answered, "Oh, yes, William. I would be happy and proud to be your wife. I love you, too."

At her words, Darcy withdrew something small from his pocket. Opening the box, he removed a ring and placed it on Elizabeth's hand. A gasp escaped as Elizabeth looked at the square-cut emerald ring. Two diamonds bordered the sides of the center stone with another diamond centered between them where it met the band.

"It is beautiful, William."

"The way the ring sparkles in the light reminds me of your eyes."

Finally, Darcy stood and drew her up with him. He raised her hand to his lips and kissed it before leaning down to kiss the tears from her cheeks. Then he gently placed his lips on hers in a tender first kiss. After a few more kisses, they returned to the house via the door to the conservatory. At the sound of the door opening, the other newly engaged couple sprang apart, having been involved in a similar activity. The two couples shared the news first with each other and basked in their shared joy. Since neither couple wished to wait, they agreed to begin the calling of the banns on the upcoming Sunday.

When the couples returned to the drawing room, Mrs. Bennet's eagle eye quickly spotted the rings on her daughters' fingers. Jane had received a beautiful sapphire and diamond ring from Bingley. Mrs. Bennet grasped Jane's and

Elizabeth's hands and raised both to better examine their rings.

"Oh, I knew you could not be so beautiful for nothing, Jane. How lucky we are that Mr. Bingley leased Netherfield Park and brought Mr. Darcy along with him. Though I cannot understand what attracted Mr. Darcy to you, Lizzy, you have done well for yourself and your family. Oh, the jewels, pin money, and carriages you will have!"

Elizabeth blushed at her mother's thoughtless words. Darcy's eyes flashed with anger, though he restrained himself from releasing it, as he realized his future mother by marriage did not mean any actual offense.

However, Darcy could not let an insult to his wife-to-be pass. "I must remember to thank Mr. Bennet, for what caught my attention was her brilliant mind. I have never enjoyed conversing so much with another as I do with Miss Elizabeth. Ours will be a great marriage." Elizabeth blushed at her betrothed's words, but the look she gave him promised a proper thank you in the future when they were once again alone.

EPILOGUE

THESE TWO DEAR SISTERS, AND THE best friends to whom they found themselves engaged, were married in a joint ceremony one month after the new year. The Darcys secluded themselves at Darcy house for three weeks, at which point Elizabeth and Lady Matlock began to shop for the clothes Elizabeth would need for the upcoming season. The Bingleys spent their first three weeks in Bath before joining the Darcys in London. After making all the necessary preparations, and with the support of the Matlocks, Elizabeth Darcy and Jane Bingley took the ton by storm. There was no one to rival Jane's classic beauty. Elizabeth's sparkling personality, vivacity, and wit won her legions of admirers as well.

The Bingleys did not renew the lease on Netherfield Park. They stayed at Pemberley until they found an estate not fifteen miles from Pemberley that suited them perfectly. The families often visited back and forth. The many cousins grew up to be the best of friends.

After accepting that Darcy would never marry her, Miss Bingley returned to London and threw herself into the season. For some time, she had finagled invitations to events in the ton by using her connection to Darcy. Upon her return to town Caroline assumed those same invitations would be available to her. However, as the information contained in Lady Matlock's notes to her dear friends made its way through the highest levels of society, the invitations Caroline Bingley so craved failed to arrive. Panicked at the thought of being sent to live with her Aunt Agnes or of setting up her own establishment, Caroline reluctantly agreed to accept an offer of marriage from a landowner whose annual income was less than Hurst's four thousand a year. She achieved her goal of becoming one of the leading hostesses of society, though not at the level she expected. Caroline and her husband gratefully accepted invitations to events held by the Bingleys, as she hoped to again gain access to the first circles. However, that was not to be. After establishing herself in London society and in an attempt at family harmony, the Darcys invited the couple to one of their balls. Unfortunately, Caroline could not release her anger at Elizabeth for getting what she, Caroline, had so wanted. This fact was evident in her behavior at the ball. As a result, no further invitations from the Darcys were issued.

Several years after his reassignment, Mr. Bennet received word of Mr. Collins' death. When no other heir was found, Mr. Bennet left the house to Mary. She had expressed an interest in learning more about the estate after Elizabeth's marriage, and since she was the most intelligent and logical of his remaining unmarried daughters, as well as a spinster by choice, she would be able to provide a home for and care for her mother until Mrs. Bennet's death. The only condition was that the house, at her death, would pass to one of Elizabeth's children.

The Darcy and Bingley families grew as the years passed. William and Elizabeth had seven children, five boys and two girls. Bingley and Jane had six children. After five girls, they finally gave birth to an heir to carry on the Bingley name and estate.

Mr. Bennet often traveled to Derbyshire for surprise visits. On these occasions, he spent the majority of his time in the library and was often found reading to the Darcy children. Occasionally, Mr. Bennet brought Kitty and Lydia along. Usually, he would leave the girls with Jane and travel on to Pemberley. Then, after a week or two, he would change places with the girls. With the help of Mr. Darcy, Bingley's collection of books grew enough to make his library into an acceptable place for a sojourn.

Both Lydia's and Kitty's behavior improved as they spent less time with their mother and more time with their elder sisters and Miss Darcy, all of whom made excellent role models. As their behavior improved and their talents and maturity increased, they were eventually promised a season and made their debut alongside Georgiana Darcy.

ACKNOWLEDGMENTS

Many thanks to my sister-in-law, Lori Whitlock, (www.loriwhitlock.com) for all her help with past covers and for creating a template that will allow me to make my own covers in the future.

Thanks also to Tonya Bluston, my wonderful editor, for her efforts at making my books error-free.

OTHER BOOKS BY LINDA C. THOMPSON

HER UNFORGETTABLE LAUGH
Her Unforgettable Laugh Series, Book 1
A Pride and Prejudice Variation

Dark curls and an unforgettably sweet laugh are all he knows of his sister's rescuer. Later, a second glimpse shows her to be lovely, and he hears her melodious laugh again. Darcy wonders what it would be like to meet this remarkable—and remarkably lovely—young woman. Would the spirit that compelled her to assist a stranger bring some joy into his lonely life? Would they ever meet? Or will he always be left wondering?

Little does Fitzwilliam Darcy know that his trip to Hertfordshire will bring him face to face with the lovely young woman whose unforgettable laugh has haunted his dreams for the last several years. Will she be anything like the woman he has built up in his dreams? Will he be able to avoid

Miss Bingley long enough to discover more about this mysterious young woman?

Laughter Through Trials
Her Unforgettable Laugh Series, Book 2
A Pride and Prejudice Variation

Dark curls and an unforgettably sweet laugh . . .

In Book 1 of the Her Unforgettable Laugh series, a trip to Hertfordshire brought Fitzwilliam Darcy face to face with the woman who had haunted his dreams for five years. Their chance meeting led to a courtship, despite the efforts of those who wished to separate them. Now Elizabeth Bennet is traveling to London, where she will be introduced to Darcy's family and the ton. How will Elizabeth be received? Will their love flourish and grow? Or will new trials overwhelm them?

THE LAUGHTER OF LOVE
Her Unforgettable Laugh Series, Book 3
A Pride and Prejudice Variation

Dark curls and an unforgettably sweet laugh . . .

In Book 2 of the Her Unforgettable Laugh series, Darcy and Elizabeth celebrated their courtship as Elizabeth was introduced to the Fitzwilliam family and London society. Their sojourn in town presented a few difficulties. However, the strength of their love allowed them to face their challenges and outwit their enemies.

Now Darcy and Elizabeth are returning to Hertfordshire for their wedding. Elizabeth worries about the one trial they have yet to face: Mrs. Bennet. Her mother refuses to prepare the simple, elegant affair the couple wishes for their wedding day. Will it be the day of their dreams ... or a disaster?

Ultimately, the wedding turns out and Darcy and Elizabeth are excited to begin their life together. The bright future before them fills their hearts with joy. Both know that they will face periods of contentment and heartache; however, united, they will confront whatever comes their way. Will those whom they have previously encountered allow them to enjoy their happiness? Or must they overcome more misfortune?

THE COMPANION'S SECRET
A Pride and Prejudice Variation

"You must marry her," the stern voice said. "I need to gain control of her inheritance before she reaches her next birthday. It need not be a long marriage, but marry her you must."

Alone in the world, Elizabeth Bennet has had to rely upon herself. She knows that escape is the only way to ensure her safety. With the help of Longbourn's faithful servants, Elizabeth disappears from her home and the odious heir. She is determined to find a way to support herself and remain hidden until after her birthday.

Fortune smiles on Elizabeth when a series of events offers her the role of companion to Georgiana Darcy. Despite her position, Elizabeth finds herself attracted to her new employer. Can he ever see her as more than his sister's companion? Sometimes, Elizabeth thinks that Mr. Darcy cares for her, too. Yet will his attraction—if that is, indeed, what he feels—survive when he learns the truth about her?

Hidden away at Pemberley, will Elizabeth be able to safely conceal herself until she comes of age? What surprises does the future hold in store for her?

A MATTER OF TIMING
A Pride and Prejudice Variation

They say that timing is everything . . .

Their chance meeting at Pemberley helps Elizabeth Bennet realize her true feelings for Mr. Darcy. That same meeting gives him the opportunity to show Elizabeth that he has taken her criticism to heart and made improvements to his behavior. Will this new start finally lead to their happily ever after?

How might the relationship between Elizabeth and Darcy have been different if they had become betrothed before Elizabeth learned of Lydia's elopement? Would they have traveled to London together? Would Elizabeth have helped with her sister's recovery? Would Lydia and Wickham still have married? Or would Elizabeth have found another way to save her youngest sister?

A Matter of Timing answers all these questions and more.

AN ACCIDENT AT PEMBERLEY
A Pride and Prejudice Variation

In the time before Mr. Bingley takes up residence at Netherfield Park, Elizabeth travels into Derbyshire with her Aunt and Uncle Gardiner. One day, as her friends and relations visit with some of Mrs. Gardiner's childhood friends, Elizabeth explores the small village. Without realizing it, she strays farther and farther from the village, unconsciously walking in the direction of Pemberley, the estate that the group had visited two days prior.

Lost in her thoughts and the beauty of the Derbyshire countryside, Elizabeth fails to notice the storm clouds building above her. At the first flash of lightning and peal of thunder, she seeks shelter from the storm, Rushing for a dense tree line where she might avoid the impending rain, Elizabeth Bennet meets with a dreadful accident.

Returning from business in London, Fitzwilliam Darcy races across the grounds of Pemberley, trying to outrun the storm. After coming across a beautiful young woman who has been injured, he takes her home so that his staff can care for her. Darcy hopes her presence will help lift his mother's melancholy.

When Elizabeth regains consciousness, she has no memory of her name or her past. During the many weeks of her recovery, Elizabeth grows close to Mr. Darcy and his mother, Lady Anne. When Elizabeth recovers enough to leave the estate, the Darcys decide that she needs an identity that will protect her from gossip. And so, Miss Elizabeth Chamberlayne, a long-lost Darcy cousin, is born. After receiving two requests, Darcy accepts an invitation to stay with his friend, Mr. Bingley, at Netherfield Park. The ladies will join him.

What will happen when Elizabeth comes face to face with her family? Will she remember them? Or will her memory still be a blank? All the original characters in Jane Austen's *Pride and Prejudice* make an appearance. How will Elizabeth's lack of memory affect her interactions with them?

A TURN IN THEIR DANCE
A Pride and Prejudice Variation

After overhearing Mr. Darcy's cutting remark at the Meryton assembly, Miss Elizabeth Bennet replies with a comment of her own about the sign of a true gentleman. When Darcy hears the statement, he is instantly stricken with remorse. He seeks a quiet place to compose himself and prepare an apology. As Miss Elizabeth moves through the crowd to share the incident with her friend, Charlotte Lucas, she hears an anguished voice from the darkened balcony. Stepping forward to offer assistance, she is surprised at what else she hears.

This event and the turn it makes in the relationship between Darcy and Elizabeth is the premise of this delightful new story. How will an earlier understanding between our dear couple change their interactions with those around them—particularly Miss Bingley, Mr. Wickham, and Mr. Collins?

www.ingramcontent.com/pod-product-compliance
Lightning Source LLC
Chambersburg PA
CBHW022122170626
46808CB00002B/820